I LOVE YOU
GUYS!!!

BLESSINGS!

Aloha

7·11·10

Katie Trout
Odd One Out

Grate Expectations

by

Coletta Kloha

INFINITY
PUBLISHING.COM

Copyright © 2009 by Coletta Kloha

ISBN 0-7414-5484-X

Published by:

INFI(∞)ITY
PUBLISHING.COM

1094 New DeHaven Street, Suite 100
West Conshohocken, PA 19428-2713
Info@buybooksontheweb.com
www.buybooksontheweb.com
Toll-free (877) BUY BOOK
Local Phone (610) 941-9999
Fax (610) 941-9959

Printed in the United States of America

Published July 2009

Dedication

D.
mashed potatoes and gravy
coffee and cream
you and me
always
C.

Chapter 1

"Sometimes I just don't know what to do with you, Katelyn!" her mother half-smiled as she opened the door to Katie's room. "I have been calling you for ten minutes to get your hind end downstairs to do your chores, and here I find you relaxing with a book. I am sooo for you being crazy about reading, but you have to do it AFTER your chores. Got it?"

Katie nodded at her mom and put the bookmark in her book. She knew her mom wasn't mad--her mom never really got mad at her—just a little exasperated at times. Like any kid, if Katie had to choose between hearing her parents yell or laugh, she would choose laughter. Katie always enjoyed hearing her parents laugh, but it seemed like during the last year or so there had been a whole lot less of it. She wouldn't have realized it so much, but both of her parents had really loud laughs, and she knew that she didn't hear the laughing as much as she used to. Katie was only eleven, but she was smart, and she knew why her parents didn't laugh as much. After her brother was born, Mom and Dad had decided that Mom should not go back to her job as a teacher. They had always wanted to start their own business together as caterers—people that made food and served it for all kinds of events. That was a really good dream because Katie's mom was a really good cook.

When her brother, Neil, was about a year old, their catering business, Caterosities, really started booming. Mom and Dad came up with the name because it reminded them of the word "curiosities" and they both thought it sounded clever and would draw interest. Mom would cook all day for grown up parties in the evenings, business meetings, and all sorts of stuff; then Dad would come home from his job managing the seafood restaurant on the other side of Beech Grove, and load up the van with all the food. If Katie's homework was done, and she didn't feel like going to the babysitter's with her brother, she would dress like Mom and Dad—white shirt, black pants, black shoes—and go with them to help serve the food. She usually did this whenever she could, because she liked hanging out with her parents and

1

helping. And the fact that they paid her $3.00 an hour (on top of her regular allowance) was pretty great, too.

Katie popped off the bed and rushed down the stairs to zip through her chores as fast as she could so that she could get back to the book she was reading. It was an old Hardy Boys mystery. She loved them, but she wished she could find a really, really amazing mystery. Usually the ones she read were pretty easy to figure out.

As Katie pulled the clean dishes out of the dishwasher and put them away, folded the mountain of towels in the laundry room, took out the garbage, fed the dog, and practiced her piano lesson, her mind was on the book she was more than half done with. And by the time Katie had dusted the living room, she was pretty sure she had solved the whole darn thing. She couldn't wait to see if she was right.

After her chores were done, and just as Katie was about to head back to her room, her mom stopped her. "Hey kiddo, you did a really great job on the chores, and I know you're anxious to get back to that book, but I was just thinking that since it's Saturday, you might want to go outside for a while to play."

This was something that Katie's mom said a lot. Mrs. Trout wasn't grumpy about it, and Katie knew that she just wanted her to get a little sunshine and hang out with some friends, but when her mom asked her if she wanted to "go out and play," it always irked Katie just a bit.

First of all, eleven year olds don't "go out and play" — that's what little kids do. Second, even if Katie wanted to, there was really no one for her to hang out with. On Saturday mornings when the weather was nice, there were always kids at the school playground a block and a half away playing baseball or basketball or just goofing around. Katie never felt like she fit in with those kids. Most of them were really nice, and she knew that they would probably include her in a game if she asked. But she also knew that they all liked to win when they played, and she knew that there wasn't one sport that she could help anyone win at. She had proof — since second grade she was always one of the last two kids chosen for a team in gym class. The only person ever chosen

2

after her was Hunter Thorne, and that was because he was really, really mean to the other kids, and he loved to push people down on the ground whenever he got the chance. Hunter probably would have gotten chosen sooner when teams were picked if he acted nicer. Katie was certain that she was dead last when it came to "ball" ability and anything that required running. It didn't matter what the game was-- kickball, softball, basketball, volleyball, dodge ball. Katie despised anything with the word "ball" attached. So, no, Katie really had no desire to "go out and play."

"No thanks, Mom, I'd rather finish my book."

Mrs. Trout looked at Katie for a moment with a mixture of love and concern. "O.K., but here's the deal—as soon as the book is finished, you get your hind end down here and you and I will take Neil and Diamond for a long walk." Mrs. Trout gave an unexpected snort of a laugh and said, "That just cracks me up every time I put their names together in the same sentence."

Katie didn't really get the joke, but she got the gist of it. Apparently there was a famous singer with the name Neil Diamond that her Mom and Dad enjoyed listening to when they were younger. Even though she didn't get the joke, she was glad to hear her mom chuckle.

Katie finished her book in less than an hour. She had been right. She had figured out how the death threats had been left in the room with no windows and only one door with a time lock to which only one person knew the combination. Katie always felt a sense of accomplishment when she could solve the mystery. Since Katie had been about five, she had thought that she would like to be a photographer when she grew up, but lately, she had been thinking that she would like to be a detective. Katie wasn't positive that she would be as good at it in real life as she was in her books. What she needed was a "practice" mystery to solve.

Little did Katie know that her chance to solve a mystery was closer than she could have ever possibly imagined.

Chapter 2

The last two nights Katie had slept miserably, and for the life of her, she couldn't figure out why. She had gone to bed on Saturday really tired—she and Mom had taken Neil and Diamond for a two mile walk, then they had come back, and headed to the grocery store. When Katie had gone to bed, she knew what that saying meant "asleep before your head hit the pillow," but in the morning she felt really groggy and grumpy.

After church on Sunday, the Trouts had gone to see a movie that Katie had been dying to see, but she was so tired that she almost fell asleep in the middle of it. Then they had stopped at Uncle Tim's house. Katie had spent the rest of the afternoon more or less entertaining Neil and their cousin, Allyson, so that the grownups could talk. Katie didn't mind playing with the two toddlers usually—they were pretty fun to be around, but today she wasn't really in the mood.

Katie went to bed exhausted again, and on Monday morning she felt absolutely no better.

"Are you feeling all right?" Mrs. Trout asked when Katie showed up at the table later than usual for breakfast with her brown hair smooshed in tangles all around her face.

"I'm O.K." Katie replied, without much enthusiasm, "just tired."

"You might be coming down with something —there is a nasty flu bug going around school, I heard -- stomachaches, fever, pukes, diarrhea, the whole nine yards. Maybe you should stay home."

"Thanks for the visual with my pancakes," Katie chuckled. "I'm fine—besides today is art and library. I don't want to miss those."

Katie managed to get herself together and to school on time. Library and art were both at the very end of the day, so Katie thought it would be quite a chore to get through the first three-quarters of the school day. It wasn't that she didn't like the kids in her class. She did, and she really did get along well with everybody (with the exception of Hunter Thorne). Her classmates—the boys <u>and</u> the girls, all seemed to really like each other. They really didn't get into arguments over dumb things like who was whose best friend and who stole whose colored pencils. Everyone did like Katie—she just wasn't at the top of the list when it came to sports, and that was just a matter of fact.

As soon as Katie walked into her classroom, though, she had the sneaking suspicion that today was going to be different than most days. Ms Carone, Katie's homeroom, English, and history teacher, had moved another desk next to Katie's. Katie's had been the last desk on the right in the third row, but now it was the second to last. Ms Carone flipped her long, chestnut brown hair over her shoulder as she made a chart on the board and filled it in with the three branches of government and their responsibilities. At the same time she explained to the class that in a few minutes they would be getting a new classmate. She was from Deerfield—the next town to the north. Maybe today would be better than Katie had anticipated.

Jordan Bailey asked, "Why did she move only one town away?"

"Well," Ms Carone answered as she turned to face the class and flip her hair once more, "I don't know that she has moved at all. I do know that her name is Talia and that she may be a little overwhelmed by everything new here, and that she will need some friends. It is our job to make her feel welcome. I know that you may have questions for her, but go a little easy on her. You'll learn more about her as time goes on. After all, that's the kindness we offered to you when you first arrived here, Jordan."

Jordan was a nice boy, but a little too "in your face" with questions sometimes. But Ms Carone was very good at keeping him and the other few students who could get off track in line. She was the kind of teacher that Katie imagined a lot of boys had a crush on: tall and pretty with a radiant smile and a quiet voice

6

and eyes that paid attention to you when you spoke and made you feel like what you were saying was important.

Just as Ms Carone finished talking to the class, there was a soft tap on the door. It was Mrs. Tyler, the principal. She escorted Talia to the front of the room.

"Classroom 5C, give a great big Beech Grove welcome to Talia Blackwitt, your new classmate," Mrs. Tyler boomed. Mrs. Tyler was the shortest woman that Katie had ever known. She was about Katie's height, and Katie was only eleven. But Mrs. Tyler had one of the biggest voices that Katie had ever heard. She more than made up for her height with her voice, and she had a reputation for being very tough, but fair. Last week, everyone had heard that Tom Scarmore, who was rumored to be the biggest sixth grader in the state of Ohio, had gotten caught smoking a cigarette in the boys' bathroom. Mrs. Tyler had given him such a talking to that it made the six foot tall two-hundred pound boy cry.

There was a modest commotion of welcome after Mrs. Tyler introduced Talia. Talia had long blonde hair and a pretty smile. She was taller than most of the girls in 5C, but then again, so was Katie. She wore a yellow sweater and blue jeans. She had on the same tennis shoes as Katie. She was going to sit next to Katie. Katie couldn't help but think that maybe they were meant to be friends.

Talia took her seat, and Katie whispered hi to her. Talia smiled back. Just then, as Mrs. Tyler left, Ms Carone came over to Katie.

"Katie, I put Talia's seat here for a reason. I knew that you would be the perfect person to show her the ropes. Make sure to answer any questions she has. You can push your desks a bit closer together—just for today. I'll send you to lunch a few minutes early so that you can show her where the restroom is and how we do the lunch line, all right?"

It was more than all right with Katie. Suddenly the tiredness from two nights of not sleeping well vanished. She felt excited at the possibility of a new friendship.

The day had been turning out rather well for Katie. Talia seemed really nice, and both of them had gotten a few extra privileges since Katie was showing around the new girl. Since they had gotten to go to lunch early, they were at the front of the lunch line. The lunch ladies gave the two of them an extra brownie each. They got to go to the library five minutes early, too, and had already checked their books out when their class came in. For once, Katie didn't have to push through the aisles with twenty-six other kids.

At recess after library, Katie, for the first time in quite a long time, had someone to hang around with. Talia didn't seem to be one for group games either, although Katie guessed by her build that she would probably be a really fast runner and be good at any "ball" game. Instead, they just walked around the playground and talked. Katie pointed out kids that were nice, and she made a point to show Talia who Hunter Thorne was so that she would be sure to keep her distance from him. They talked about music that they liked, books that they had read, their brothers (Talia had two older ones), and their favorite movies.

When recess was over, Katie felt like they had a lot in common, and she thought that her first instinct was definitely right—she had a new friend.

Finally, it was time for art class. Mrs. Stemple had told them last week that today each student would be making a design on a piece of thin copper by pressing a nail down firmly onto it. They were supposed to have come up with a design before class today. Katie had decided to make an emblem for Caterosities as a surprise for her mom. She had even asked Mrs. Stemple the size of the copper so that when she had a little time on the computer when Mom wasn't paying attention, she could print off the name of the business in a cool font. She had found a nice clip-art picture of two chili peppers, and had printed that off behind the name. All she had to do now was line it up on the copper and poke through her paper to dent the copper all the way around the outlines.

When Katie took her design up to show Mrs. Stemple, the teacher was really impressed. "Good gracious, Katie, that is one heck of a design! Your parents are absolutely going to love it."

The teacher went on to announce to the class, "Katie brought in a design for her copper project — did anyone else?" After a long pause, she continued, "I thought not. Did any of you even bother to come up with the foggiest notion of what you are going to make today?"

No one looked at Mrs. Stemple, so with a big sigh she began passing out pieces of paper and pencils for the students to use for their rough drafts. "Remember, you have to plan this out since you will only get ONE piece of copper."

Hunter Thorne yelled out a question. "Do we get to keep the nail?"

Mrs. Stemple knew Hunter well. She said, "Absolutely not. In fact, Hunter, yours is the first one that I will collect at the end of class."

Katie got two nails and two pieces of copper, — one set for her and one set for Talia. Since Talia hadn't been there the week before, and she didn't like to draw, she was clueless as to what to create. Katie helped her draw a design of big chunky letters on paper that said "Talia's Room" — a sign for her bedroom door. Talia loved the idea and got to work quickly with pushing her nail. Both girls kept talking as they created their copper works of art.

Katie was curious whether Talia had moved from Deerfield or if she stilled lived there. It was only about a seven minute drive away. Katie figured that since she and Talia had a lot in common and had been talking all day, she might as well just ask, but she wanted to do it in such a was as to not seem too nosy.

"Talia, will the sign you are making go on a new door or an old door?"

"What do you mean?" Talia asked as she looked up from lining up her design with her piece of copper.

"I mean, are you going to be putting it on the same bedroom door you've always had, or did you just move here and now you have a new door to put it on?"

"Oh," Talia hesitated just a bit, but continued as she started to use her nail to poke through her paper. "It's a new door. We had a pretty big house in Deerfield, but we had to sell it because my dad's business isn't doing so well. We had to buy a smaller house that was still around here, so that Dad would be close to the restaurant, and Mom would be close to her job at the hospital. Dad said that he didn't want all the money we get from selling the old house to be spent in gas money to get back and forth to work from a long distance. Our new house is all right, but I liked the old one a lot better. I'm lucky. I still get my own room since I'm the only girl. Jimmy and Jory, my brothers, used to have their own rooms, but now they have to share — and now they fight a lot more because of it. I wanted to keep going to my old school, but since Mom had to go back to work, and Dad goes to work early, and Jimmy and Jory leave earlier for school since they're older, Dad said I'd be doing my part to help the family if I didn't put up a fight about this. Beech Grove Elementary is closer to our house and is right on Mom's way to work. It worked out that she could just drop me off every morning here, instead of going seven minutes one way to my old school in Deerfield and then seven minutes back to Beech Grove and then five more minutes to work.

"I was really mad, and asked them both if they didn't think my happiness was worth fourteen minutes a day. Mom and Dad didn't say anything when I asked that, probably because I didn't give them a chance. I just stormed out and ran over to Robyn's house. She's my best friend that lives — lived — three houses away.

"I talked to Robyn and calmed down. I knew the decision wasn't up to me anyway. Mom and Dad would do whatever they decided that they were going to do. I didn't say anything more to them about it. And here we are."

Talia wasn't mad as she told Katie all this, just matter of fact. It made Katie feel very sad for her new friend. She couldn't even imagine how upset she would be if her family suddenly decided to move away, even if it wasn't very far.

All Katie could think to say as they continued to press their nails into the copper was, "I'm sorry that all this has happened to you. I'd be — I don't know how I'd feel, to tell the truth, but I bet I'd feel just like you do. Is Robyn nice?"

Talia answered quickly, "Oh, yeah. She's really funny. She loves to play practical jokes. One time she made this brown paint and glue mixture and let it dry like a puddle, and then she put it with an empty pop can on top of her dad's business papers. It really did look like pop had spilled all over the place. He was really mad. . ."

Talia's voice drifted off. She was staring at Katie's finished design. Katie hadn't bothered to show it to her before because they were so busy trying to make the quick rough draft for Talia.

"What is that?" Talia asked in a really weird voice — kind of frightened almost.

"I made a little, heck, I don't know what you'd call it, a plaque, maybe, for my mom and dad's catering business. Mom's birthday is coming up. I think I might see if I can dig up an old picture frame around the house, clean it up, and frame this for a gift. What do you think?"

Talia was still staring at Katie's Caterosities design with the chili peppers. Her mouth was pinched shut tight and she had a strange look on her face. When Talia didn't answer Katie's question, Katie pushed her copper closer so that Talia could see it better just as the bell rang.

Talia pushed it right back to Katie and stood up. The class was pushing their chairs in. Mrs. Stemple was standing right beside Hunter with her hand out to collect his nail.

In a quiet, angry voice, Talia suddenly whispered, "You are the reason I had to move. I didn't realize it until just now. Of all the people in all the world, I had to get paired up with you. You are <u>not</u> my friend."

Chapter 3

Katie sat stunned in the empty art room. She was relieved that the day was over and she only had to go to her locker and head for home. Katie didn't want anyone to see the tears that were burning so badly in her eyes.

The lights were still on in the art room. Mrs. Stemple must have gone somewhere when the kids left, but she must be coming back. Katie didn't want Mrs. Stemple to see her crying. Katie wiped her face with the sleeve of her shirt, took a deep breath, and headed to her locker. Enough time had passed that just about everyone had cleared out of the school. If she took her time, she would miss the crossing guards, too. She didn't want them to see her upset either.

Katie put her math book and her homework folder in her backpack. Then she pulled the math book back out. She opened it and placed the "Caterosities" plaque between the pages, so it wouldn't get bent on the way home. Before she closed the book, she looked at it for a minute.

Everything had been fine with Talia until she saw Katie's piece of copper. What had Talia said? Katie was the reason she had to move? How was that possible? Katie had never even seen Talia before today. What in the world did Talia think Katie had done?

The school day that had started out great had ended more miserably than any other day she had ever had.

Katie had been startled and sad when Talia had spoken to her like that, but now her feelings were changing. She felt angry. She knew that she hadn't done anything—anything except be completely kind to the new girl all day long.

Katie grabbed her coat, but didn't bother to put it on. She slammed the locker door, ran up the steps, and slammed through the side door of the building. Katie really had to talk to someone about this.

Her mom and dad had always told her that when she had a problem, she could talk to them about it no matter what. Katie knew that it was true, and that that was exactly what she planned to do.

As Katie walked the block and a half home by herself, she thought about what she would tell her parents about her day — how it had started out great with Katie thinking that just maybe she had finally found a friend that she had something in common with, but then the day suddenly--boy, did that seem like an understatement — it seemed a whole lot quicker than "sudden," that Talia had changed from really nice to unbelievably mean.

As Katie walked, she started to calm down, and she tried really hard to breathe normally. She knew that she hadn't done anything wrong. This was all some kind of weird misunderstanding. Mom and Dad were both pretty good about solving problems. She really couldn't decide who she would rather talk to about this. Maybe both of them at the same time — three heads were better than just one.

By the time she got home, Katie realized that she wasn't feeling as sad or angry as she had been a few minutes earlier. Now she just felt confused. Unfortunately, neither of her parents was at home. The note on the table said, "Katie, there are some extra homemade taquitos for the party at the Callahans tonight in the frig. Have a couple for a snack, and then do your chores and homework. Neil and I should be back from setting up by about 4:00. Dad might beat me home. You can go with us tonight if you want — it's up to you. If you are going to go, you have to be ready by 5:00. Love, Mom"

Katie had expected that at least one of her parents would be there when she got home, but she didn't waste any more time crying. She started on her usual chores, but decided that first, it might be a good idea to let Diamond outside for a few minutes while she filled his bowl with food and changed his water. The little puffball was bouncing up and down by the door as if he might explode at any second. Katie took the clean dishes out of the dishwasher and put them away. She could hear Diamond barking happily in the yard, even though all the windows and doors were shut. After that, Katie headed for the dryer. She hoped that it was towels to be folded. Those were the quickest and the easiest. Instead, she found a load of socks and underwear. That figured! That was Katie's absolute least favorite chore in the world—matching socks! Katie couldn't wait until Neil was old enough to have some chores, but who was she kidding, he was only two years old. He couldn't even use the toilet yet, let alone help out around the house.

Just as Katie finished, Dad came in with two bags of groceries. He looked a little tired. Maybe she shouldn't dump the whole "Talia" thing on him right now, Katie thought.

"Hey Cutes!" Dad said as he started to put the groceries away. "How was your day?"

Katie couldn't truthfully say that it had been good, so she just shrugged instead. Suddenly she realized that she hadn't heard Diamond barking for a few minutes.

"Where are you off to?" Dad yelled after her as she grabbed the doorknob.

"I'm just going to let Diamond in, then you can tell me about your day." Katie thought she had done a pretty good job of changing the subject from her day to dad's.

Katie whistled for Diamond to come back inside, but he didn't make his usual dash for the door. She called him again, but there was still no sign of him. Katie closed the door behind her and went out into the fenced in back yard to see what he was up to.

As soon as she stepped into the grass, she saw it. On the far side of the yard was a little mound of dirt. Katie ran over to it. There was a hole—just the right size for Diamond to fit through— that went under the fence and into the Kimballs' yard.

"DAD!! COME OUT HERE!!!" Katie shrieked at the top of her lungs. The sobs began as she saw her dad running toward her through the yard. He immediately saw what was wrong, knelt down beside her, and grabbed her by the shoulders and began saying the words Katie really hoped were true.

"I am sure that Diamond is fine. He just needed a little adventure." Mr. Trout hugged Katie for a moment, and said, "Now, let's be smart about this. He couldn't have gotten far. I'll call Mom on her cell phone to let her know what's going on, and I'll head over to the Kimball's. After that, I'll head across the street, and go toward the school. That is probably the direction he headed since the hole is on that side of the yard, and you know how he loves to listen to the kids playing on the playground. I want you to start knocking on the doors of our neighbors on this side of the street, and ask if they've seen Diamond. Only stop at the houses of the people we know. Meet me back here in fifteen minutes, and if we haven't found him, we'll decide what to do from there. Got it?"

Katie just nodded as she got up off the ground. Dad opened the gate, and they both headed out. Dad went right next door, and Katie ran to the house on the other side of the Kimballs. The Walshs lived there, but no one answered the front door. Katie ran around to the back yard, just in case Mr. or Mrs. Walsh was out by the garage. There was no sign of Diamond, and when she peeked in the garage window, she saw that both of the Walshs' vehicles were not there. She made a mental note to make sure to call them when she got home and leave a message on their answering machine so that they could keep an eye out for Diamond. But then again, maybe she wouldn't have to—maybe she would find Diamond any minute.

Katie ran to the next house. The McKeevers lived there. Mr. McKeever was Katie's math, science and computer teacher, but he wasn't home either. He was probably still at school grading papers.

The next house was very pretty. The new owners had painted it gray and it had blue shutters. The problem was that Katie couldn't remember their name—was it Marthey? Matheny?--she was sure her mom had told it to her—and Katie hadn't met them yet. If they were in the front yard, she thought it would be okay to talk to them, but they weren't, and she knew Dad wouldn't want her to go to the door, since she didn't know them.

Katie had checked three houses and still hadn't talked to anyone. Finally, as she rang the bell at Mrs. Portage's house, and heard a faint "I'm coming," she felt some relief. Mrs. Portage opened the door and smiled at Katie.

"Well, what brings you here, little one?" Mrs. Portage said as she pushed the wisps of gray hair out of her eyes with the back of her flour-covered hand. Katie found it funny that Mrs. Portage always called her "little one" because Katie certainly was not little. Katie wondered if Mrs. Portage always said that because she couldn't actually remember Katie's name.

"Did you smell the cookies, and suddenly realized that you were in terrible need of an after school snack?"

Katie answered quickly, all the words tumbling out. "No, Mrs. Portage, but thank you. I'm here because my dog Diamond dug a hole under our fence and has run away. I was wondering if you had seen him. It happened in the last twenty minutes or so. He's brown, and fluffy, about this big, and barks a lot."

Mrs. Portage grabbed Katie's outstretched hands that were demonstrating the size of Diamond. Katie could feel the dryness of Mrs. Portage's floury hands clasping Katie's sweaty palms.

"No I haven't, sweetie, but I'll keep my eye out! Is this the first time he's done this?"

"Yes! I am so scared that he's going to get hit or not be able to find his way home!"

"Take a breath, little one. Dogs have a good sense of direction. He'll be able to find his way back. Don't you worry. And we live in a very quiet neighborhood. Cars drive really slowly through here because of all the signs that warn about children playing." Mrs. Portage spoke reassuringly as she squeezed Katie's hands. She didn't even seem to notice that the mixture of flour and sweat was getting very gluey.

"Yeah. Dad was heading over to the school to see if Diamond is there. He loves to be around kids." Mrs. Portage and Katie both looked toward the school, but because the weather was cooler today, neither of them could see any kids playing outside. Katie felt her heart sink.

It seemed to Katie that Mrs. Portage could read her thoughts, because the next thing she said was, "Well, it looks pretty quiet over there. He might have gone another direction." Katie was only able to nod.

"Little one, when you are in your yard, can you hear any other children, besides the ones outside at school?"

Katie thought for a moment. "Yes!! Two streets over from us, there is that woman who takes care of all those kids at her house. I don't know her name."

"Now you're thinking! You're right! That's Mrs. Barry. She has a day care business in her home. Are kids usually playing in her yard?"

"All the time, but maybe not today since it is colder out."

"Well, it's worth a shot, don't you think? Do you want me to come with you?" Mrs. Portage offered.

"Thank you, but I have to meet my dad back home right now. We'll try Mrs. Barry's next," Katie said as she dashed down the steps and back toward her house.

Mrs. Portage yelled after her. "Let me know what happens, and come back for some cookies!"

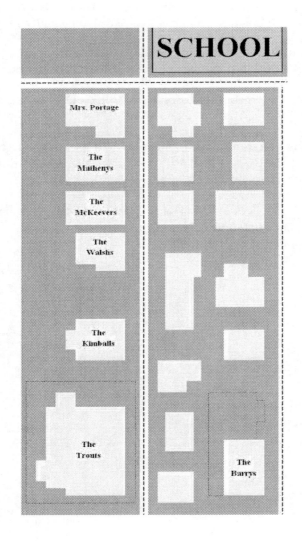

SCHOOL

Mrs. Portage

The
Mathenys

The
McKeevers

The
Walshs

The
Kimballs

The
Trouts

The
Barrys

Chapter 4

Katie stood outside the chain-link fence at Mrs. Barry's home with Diamond in her arms. Mr. Trout knelt down on the ground and peered in the direction of their house.

"Well, I'll be. . . Mrs. Portage was right! Diamond must have been plotting his escape for some time. Look there, you can see our fence from here. Diamond probably watched the kids over here every day through a gap in the fence, and then looked for an easy place to dig. When he found it, he headed right here. All that work, and there aren't even any kids out today."

Katie was just glad that Diamond was all right. When they found him, he was just laying quietly with his head on his paws. Diamond looked terribly dejected to Katie—as if the whole adventure had turned out to be a waste of his time and energy. Katie knew exactly what that felt like. Her whole experience with Talia today had been a waste. She was really bummed out, too.

Dad called Mom to let her know that Diamond had been found. Katie knew that it must be getting close to 4:30. Katie had finished her chores, except for practicing piano and doing her math homework. Katie really did want to talk to her parents about Talia, and she really didn't feel like going to the babysitter's, so as soon as she and Dad got home, she did her homework. Luckily, it was only three long division problems. She had done the other seven at school. Katie whipped through her three piano songs for the week at lightning speed, and then threw on her Caterosities clothes, so that she could help out at the party. Katie figured that since there was sometimes a lull for a few minutes here or there in the kitchen, maybe there would be an opportunity to talk to her parents then.

That was about the first thing that went as Katie had planned all day. When her mom leaned back against the counter and reached for her diet soda, she knew that this was her chance to get their advice. Katie knew that the lull wouldn't last long, so she didn't waste any time.

"Mom, Dad, something happened today at school that was really . . . cruddy."

Immediately, Mom put down her can and Dad stopped counting forks. "Are you all right?" they both said in unison. Mom and Dad were always quick to defend Katie, since they knew that she wasn't one to start trouble—in fact, she liked to avoid it whenever possible.

"Yeah, I'm okay, but there was a new girl that started today. . ." and Katie began to recount Talia's entry into Katie's class, the fact that Katie was assigned to show her around and that they seemed to have a lot in common. Katie explained how she had helped Talia all day and how things had seemed fine until the end of art class when all of the sudden Talia started blaming Katie for stuff that Katie knew nothing about.

Dad immediately dropped the handful of forks he was holding. The crash they made as they hit the forks he had already counted was pretty loud, but Dad didn't seem to care. "This girl, Talia . . . her last name doesn't happen to be Blackwitt, does it, Katie?" Dad asked in a voice that seemed on the verge of being angry.

"Yeah, Dad. That is her last name. How did you know?"

"Oh, honey, I'm sorry. Talia is a very unusual name—and it happens to be the name of Simon's youngest child."

"You mean the guy you used to work for? Simon's last name is Blackwitt?" Katie couldn't believe it.

"I'm afraid so. I had heard that they recently moved, but I didn't know where. I figured it was because of money trouble and that he had sold Oceanview. He was not an easy guy to work for." Katie's dad shook his head.

"Talia told me that they moved because her dad's business wasn't going well and they needed a smaller house, probably to save money. I guess she figured out who I was when she read "Caterosities" on the present I was making you in art class."

"You remember it wasn't long after we started Caterosities that I decided to quit my manager's job at Oceanview and work with your mom full time. Mom really did need the help. Things seemed really great for a while, but then business started to slow down—a lot. At first we thought it was because of the economy, and that maybe people just weren't throwing as many parties, but then we found out that that wasn't the reason for the drop in business at all. Simon had started bad-mouthing Caterosities all over town. He was mad because I had quit my job and his business was losing money. Since he was mad at me for leaving, he decided to start telling everyone he could that Caterosities served awful food, if we showed up to serve food at all," Dad said dejectedly.

Katie knew that simply was not true. Mom and Dad had never ever not shown up when they promised, and the food was great. It made Katie so infuriated when people told lies! It made her even madder when other people believed them. Right now business was a little steadier than it had been in a while. Because of that, Mom and Dad weren't quite as worried about the money they needed to make to stay in business and to pay the bills. And when they weren't as worried, they laughed a little more—and then Katie was less worried, too.

"If Simon was mean enough to talk badly about you guys all over town, why wouldn't he talk to his daughter, too? She said I was the reason she had to move. It probably does seem that way to her if she isn't getting the whole story. She needs to know what a pain her dad is. He used to make you work all kinds of crazy hours at Oceanview. You took care of the whole place pretty much on your own, Dad. He used to hire all kinds of people because they would work for low pay, then when they didn't do the work, Simon would make you pick up the slack and fire them. Talia needs to know that her moving was not my fault, or your fault. The only person she should be blaming is her own father for treating people the way he does!" Katie sat down on the stool by the cutting board. She was angry all over again.

Dad looked at Mom. "I guess Simon isn't the only one guilty of carrying on adult conversations too often in front of the children." Mom gave him a look that showed she was as angry and confused as Katie felt.

"Look, honey, you're right," Dad said. "Simon was a tough guy to work for, and to be honest, I am glad I don't have to anymore, but I don't want you to have to put up with meanness on account of the decision your mother and I made to start this business. I can tell by that look in your eyes that you think it would be a good idea to talk to Talia about her dad, but I am going to put a stop to that thought right now. Talia will be just as protective of her father as you are of me. You are angry, and approaching Talia about this whole thing might just make things a lot worse. Let her cool off for a while. Give her some space — give yourself some space. But you have to realize that this is not your fault. Talia is angry that her life has changed and now she has found someone she thinks she can blame."

Mom looked at Katie with eyes that looked like she might cry. "If you need us to, Dad or I will go in to see Ms Carone and Mr. McKeever to let them know a little about what is going on. That way they don't continue to pair you up with Talia until things calm down."

"No, Mom. It's okay. I'll talk to them if I need to. Believe it or not, it helps just knowing why she's mad, even though I can't change it."

Just then, Mrs. Callahan stuck her head in the kitchen and told Mr. and Mrs. Trout that everyone was ready for dinner. Even though the three of them didn't feel great about what Katie was going through, all of them felt good about the fact that they were in it together and had talked about it.

Chapter 5

By the time the Trouts cleaned up after the party and picked up Neil from the babysitter's, it was already way past Katie's bedtime. Katie changed into her pajamas, kissed her parents, and headed for bed. Her body felt really tired from the exhausting day and the fact that she hadn't been sleeping well, but her mind was racing.

Katie couldn't stop thinking about how lousy the day had been—losing Diamond and Talia turning out not to be the friend she had hoped for. Katie knew that she wouldn't be able to sleep until she had some good thoughts in her head, so she focused on the fact that Diamond was safe and sound, and that it was a really great thing that she got along so well with her parents. Katie knew of a lot of kids that didn't.

Mom was finally getting Neil calmed down. He had fallen asleep at the babysitter's, and even though Dad had tried to get him in his car seat without waking him up, it hadn't worked. On the ride home Neil was really cranky, but once he got in the house, he was ready to play. This was Mom's least favorite part about having her own business. The hours weren't really regular, and it messed with Neil's sleeping schedule.

Katie could hear Mom's soothing voice and the little CD player pulsing a lullaby through the old wall. Katie felt her eyelids getting heavy. She was yawning and turning toward the opposite wall when she suddenly remembered that she hadn't told Mrs. Portage that she had found Diamond.

Katie made a mental note to leave for school a bit early in the morning and stop by Mrs. Portage's house. She wouldn't knock or ring the bell unless she heard noise inside the house since it was so early in the morning. If she didn't hear anything, she would stop right after school.

Everything was finally quiet upstairs. Katie could hear Mom and Dad downstairs talking softly. Neil's room was quiet, and

Katie had seen Diamond asleep in his bed in the living room when she had headed upstairs. Katie was glad for the peace. As she closed her eyes, though, she realized that there was a little sound that she couldn't identify.

Katie pulled the covers up over her head hoping to muffle the sound enough so that she could sleep. She kept her head under the covers for only about two minutes until she got unbelievably hot. Katie poked her head out and listened. It was still there—a fluttering, and she knew that it would drive her crazy, like a mosquito buzzing around her head, if she didn't find out what was making the noise and stop it.

Katie flicked on the light next to her bed and sat up. Only her head moved as she looked around the room. There wasn't anything flying around the room. It wasn't the sound of a cricket. It sounded more like paper fluttering. The sound was coming from over by the door, but it was definitely in her room. Katie slipped out of bed and tiptoed slowly across the carpet. She knelt down on her hands and knees by the door, and realized that the sound was coming from the heating grate. She peeked through the circles of the metal grating and saw something little and whitish flapping.

Katie hopped up and went first to her bedside table to get her flashlight and then to the bathroom to get a pair of tweezers. Then she lay down flat on her stomach in front of the grate and held the flashlight in her left hand while she gently tried to remove the piece of whatever it was with the tweezers. It was stuck on the backside of the old grate pretty well, but Katie managed to wiggle it free, and begin to pull it through the grate.

Katie usually wasn't this careful about things, but her gut was telling her to take her time—that was probably because the first peek at the paper pinched between the tweezers as it came through the grate told Katie that it was old—really old. That's because it wasn't white, it was really yellowish--like the mark a teabag leaves on a paper towel. It wasn't as small as Katie had first thought, either. It was about the size of an index card.

When Katie had pulled it out far enough to grasp it with her fingers, she realized that it had letters on it. Katie curved the paper so that it would fit through a small space in the metal circles. Finally, it slid out of the grate and into her hand.

The paper's edges were torn. She read the words—

presents

"Now and Then"

a play by Thurgood Beckett

Saturday, October 23rd

Katie was baffled. A piece of what looked like a program from a play was fluttering around in the ducts of her house for a really long time. Katie knew that their house was old, but she didn't know that it was old enough for really ancient stuff like this to be in it!

Katie held the paper gently in her hand as she got up from the floor and headed down to show Mom and Dad. When she got to the top of the stairs, she realized that all the lights were off downstairs. While she had been fishing this thing out of the grate, she must not have even noticed that Mom and Dad had come upstairs and gone to bed. Katie knew that they must already be asleep, because there was no light coming out from underneath their door.

It was really interesting, but Katie didn't think it was worth waking up her tired parents for. It could wait until breakfast. Katie tiptoed back into her room and quietly closed the door. She opened her math book and took the Caterosities sign out from between the pages and replaced it with the old piece of paper. Katie stuck her sign in the bottom dresser drawer under all her pajamas. Mom wouldn't look in there since Katie had to put all her own clean clothes away.

Katie hopped back into bed and covered up. She realized that in the last couple of nights Mom or Dad must have turned the heat up in their old drafty house since it was finally autumn and the nights were getting cooler. That must have knocked the piece of paper loose from wherever it had been stuck before. It had probably been there the last couple of nights, and that may have been why Katie hadn't been sleeping great.

Katie hoped that that was the end of that, because she certainly wanted this crazy day to end.

Chapter 6

Katie woke up feeling like she had really had a good night's sleep—even though she had gone to bed very late, and even though the Talia problem was still on her mind.

Katie hadn't decided yet how she was going to handle the whole Talia thing. She guessed it was best to take her parents' advice and not approach her. Maybe if Katie pretended yesterday had never happened, and kept her distance from Talia, everything would be okay.

Katie reached for her math book on the nightstand to take another look at the piece of paper, but before she could open it, she heard a howl come from her parents' room.

"How is it possible that the three responsible people in this house all managed to oversleep?!" Mom yelled. "That is the entire reason you and I have two alarm clocks, Dan! Did you set yours last night? Oh, forget it! I won't shower this morning since I am just going back over to the Callahans' to take down the tables. You get a shower, meet with the accountant, and then meet me at the Callahans' to load up the tables. Are you going to take Neil with you or will I? I'll take him with me. They have that little boy he can play with. It shouldn't take me more than an hour. If you aren't there when I'm done, I'll run quick to pick up more detergent for the tablecloths. Call me and we'll meet to load the tables. I'll throw the coffee on. Turn off the pot when you leave, honey."

Katie practically ran into her mom as they both came out of their bedrooms like two wild animals. Mom was wobbling on one leg as she tried to jam the other leg into her jeans.

"Katie, honey, get dressed! School starts in fifteen minutes. I'll put a bagel in the toaster for you. You might have to eat it on the way to school. I washed all your jeans last night. They're in the dryer. Did you set your clock last night? Oh, forget it! Let's get a move on!"

Mom was like a tornado. The thing that flipped her switch worse than anything was being late. Katie didn't have a chance to say a word. Mom had already disappeared into Neil's room to startle him awake and dress him.

Katie could hear the shower running, so she knew she couldn't talk to Dad right now about the piece of paper. Talking to Mom at this point was out of the question. After school might be the best bet.

Katie got dressed, combed her hair, brushed her teeth—all in record time. She hustled downstairs, put her math book in her backpack, spread cream cheese on her bagel, yelled goodbye to Mom and Dad, and headed out the door. Just as Katie got to the end of the driveway, the front door flew open and Mom ran out yelling, "Wait a minute—hang on!" She caught her breath and gave Katie a big hug.

"I am so sorry to start your day off like this. I love you. And do not let that Talia get the best of you! I'll be home when you get home, so we can talk some more, if you want."

"Okay, Mom. Try to relax a little. The world won't end if you're a few minutes late to take off some tablecloths."

"You're right. You're right!" Mom sighed. "Have a great day! You'd better get going!"

Mrs. Trout headed back in the house, and Katie picked up the pace. She remembered that she had wanted to stop at Mrs. Portage's house. Katie knew she would already be cutting it close, but she didn't want Mrs. Portage to be worried about Diamond all day. Katie decided to stop by. It probably wouldn't be that big a deal if she was a couple of minutes late for school since she hadn't been late so far this year.

Katie, the girl who hated to run almost as much as she hated games that involved the word "ball," found herself doing exactly that--past the neighboring houses and up Mrs. Portage's steps. Before she could even put her ear to the door to listen for sounds, Mrs. Portage opened the door.

"Little one, I woke up early because I thought you might stop by. Running a little late for school, aren't you? I heard the first bell already ring."

"Yep. We all overslept. I just wanted to let you know that you were right! We found Diamond sitting outside of Mrs. Barry's fence. He is just fine. Thanks for helping me think it through."

"No problem, Katie. I'm just glad it all worked out. If you have time after school, why don't you stop by? I made way too many chocolate chip cookies, and I could use a little help eating them. I believe you'll be hungry by the time school is out if that's all you are eating for breakfast," Mrs. Portage said.

"That sounds great. I'll see you then!" Katie started to walk away, but turned around. "Mrs. Portage, I found something last night, and I haven't had a chance to show it to anyone. It's something kind of odd. Do you have a second that I could show you?"

"Certainly, little one, but I don't want you to be late," Mrs. Portage replied in a concerned tone.

"It'll just take a second. Could you hold this?" Katie handed Mrs. Portage the half of the bagel as she reached into her backpack for her math book.

Katie pulled out the piece of paper and held it in front of Mrs. Portage. Mrs. Portage adjusted her glasses and put her nose very close to the piece of paper. "Well, I'll be . . . Where on earth did you get this?"

Katie quickly told her how she had retrieved it from the heating grate.

Mrs. Portage gingerly took the paper and gave Katie her bagel. "It looks like a play bill from a very long time ago. The historical society might be very interested in this."

From where Katie was standing, one step lower than Mrs. Portage, she could see that there was something written on the back side of the paper. Katie hadn't bothered to look at the other side last night.

Katie popped the last of the bagel into her mouth and pointed to the handwriting that was much more faded than the printed writing on the front. "Look at that, Mrs. Portage. Someone wrote on the other side."

"Well, I'll be. . ." Mrs. Portage said for the second time. But that was all she said for a long moment.

"My eyesight isn't the best. I can't really make it out, but I do think it looks pretty interesting. Tell you what. If you trust me Katie, I could keep it for you until after school. That way it doesn't get lost. I could also see what I could find out about this play, Now and Then. You could pick it up right after school."

Katie thought that it might be a good idea. If it was an important old paper, she didn't want to take the chance on losing it. "That's sounds fine, Mrs. P." Katie said. "I'll call my mom this afternoon from school to tell her that I'll be here for a bit this afternoon. I'll see you then."

Mrs. Portage nodded, staring again at the small, yellowed paper. "See you then, little one."

Chapter 7

Katie hadn't had time to look at the handwritten words while she was at Mrs. Portage's, and now that she was at school, that's all she could think about. She figured she was thinking about that so much to avoid thinking about Talia.

"Take your seat, Katie, and work on correcting the sentences that are on the board," Ms Carone said as Katie entered the classroom. Katie had been right. Since she was a good student, and had never been late before, Ms Carone didn't make a big deal about it, not the way she did when Hunter Thorne came into the room late, which seemed to be about every other morning.

As Katie sat down, she took a quick glance over at Talia. Their desks were no longer pushed together. Katie wondered if the janitor, Ms Carone or Talia had done that. It really didn't matter to Katie. Talia was completely ignoring her, which was fine by Katie. Katie got to work on her sentences.

By lunch, Katie had relaxed a bit about the whole Talia thing. It was not exactly comfortable to sit next to her, but the fact that both of them ignored each other completely didn't make it terrible. At least Talia wasn't being mean. Katie would like it if one of their desks got moved, but Katie would have to think about how to ask Ms Carone without Ms Carone feeling that they all needed to sit down and have a talk.

Katie asked in the office to call home at recess. She got Mom's approval to go to Mrs. Portage's house, and reassured Mom that everything was bearable with Talia. Mrs. Trout's consent for Katie to visit Mrs. Portage sent Katie's thoughts spiraling again about the paper.

There had been no year on the old paper when the play had taken place. How old was the note? Why had it been in Katie's house? She really wished that she had looked at the faded writing before she gave it to Mrs. Portage, so that she would have more to think on. Katie was thrilled when the school day was over. She found herself for the second time that day actually running--and both times had been to see Mrs. Portage.

For the second time that day, Mrs. Portage opened the door as soon as Katie reached it.

"Come in, Katie. The cookies are on the table. So is the paper. Why don't you wash your hands first? Did you remember to call your mom or do you need to call her now?" Mrs. Portage asked.

"Nope. I already called. She said that it was fine that I come over. She seemed curious about why, and I told her it was because I wanted to tell you about Diamond and that you had invited me for cookies yesterday."

"Well, that's true, but you told me about Diamond this morning. Why didn't you tell her about the paper?" Mrs. Portage asked.

"I don't know — I guess I felt like this could really be a mystery and if too many people knew it would just feel . . . ordinary. I'll tell Mom about it later, don't worry," Katie said reassuringly to Mrs. Portage.

"Little one, I think you are right about the "mystery." I was on the internet today and I called the Lindeman County Historical Society and I learned some pretty interesting things!" Mrs. Portage almost whispered with a twinkle in her eye as she motioned for Katie to sit down at the kitchen table after she had washed her hands.

"You didn't tell anyone about the note, did you?" Katie asked worriedly.

"Mercy sakes, of course not! I told the man at the historical society that I was doing some research for a book. Pretty clever, huh? Just for the heck of it, I made up a fake name for myself . . . Mrs. Pimplepuff . . . Claudia Pimplepuff, to be exact!" Mrs. Portage giggled.

"Why did you do that?" Katie asked, laughing herself.

"Oh, I guess it was because you and I were probably thinking the same thing. We don't know much about what this little old piece of paper is, but we both have a feeling that it could be important and that for now it should be kept under the rug," Mrs. Portage said winking.

"Is there a safer place?" Katie asked seriously.

"A safer place than what?" Mrs. Portage asked equally seriously.

"I mean, is there a better place to keep the paper than under the rug? If people walk all over it, it could fall apart, and if it gets vacuumed up by mistake. . ."

Mrs. Portage's laugh interrupted Katie. "Heaven's no, Katie. 'Under the rug' is an expression. It means that we need to keep this quiet for a while. But you bring up a good point. Since it might be important, where should you keep it?"

"We, Mrs. P.," Katie said. "This isn't my paper anymore, it's ours. You are the one that already thought to start researching. Your house is probably a safer place to keep it than mine. I have Neil, Diamond and a mom that occasionally goes on cleaning binges — all serious threats to a little piece of paper. I trust you completely with it . . . Mrs. Pimplepuff!" Katie said laughing loudly.

"I have a lock box in my bedroom closet. We'll keep it in there between the pages of my old diary," Mrs. Portage said as she pulled an old tin off the windowsill above the kitchen sink and shook it. Katie heard a small clanking noise. "Here is where I keep the key."

"You shouldn't be telling me your hiding places, Mrs. Portage," Katie said. "I am honored, but you don't know me very well. I could be a thief!"

"Are you?" Mrs. Portage asked her eyes wide.

"Well, no," Katie said.

"See, I already knew that." Mrs. Portage gave a big sigh and she was quiet for a minute, staring out the window above the sink into her backyard. Finally she continued, "Katie, my kids have all grown up and moved away. I don't get to see my grandkids very often. I spend a lot of time by myself. I have friends, but they never want to go anywhere or do anything. Adventure for them is an afternoon of cards and a new dessert. I have lived on this block all my adult life—I even remember when your mom and dad moved into the neighborhood before you were born. I have seen you walk to school many, many mornings. I have the feeling that you and I are a lot alike. I am the odd one out with my friends, and I'm not saying this to be hurtful, but I get the feeling that you are the odd one out, too. You are different from other kids. Some people see that as a bad thing. I choose to see it as a fantastic thing. I think I probably know a lot more about you than you think. I think you'll probably find that even though about sixty years separate us in age from each other, we're really a whole lot alike. That's why I think I can tell you where I keep my key."

Katie's eyes were filling with tears, just like Mrs. Portage's were. That was just another way they really were alike.

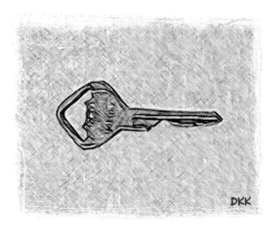

Chapter 8

"Well, little one, that's enough of that. We've got business to tend to. I have to fill you in on all of the interesting things that I found out today. Some of them I actually knew at one time, but it's been so long that I had forgotten!" Mrs. Portage's words came tumbling out as she sat down at the table and gently pushed the note toward Katie.

"Mrs. P., this piece of paper is about all I could think about all day at school. What did you find out?"

"Well, on the internet I found out that this guy, Thurgood Beckett, was a little known playwright that lived from 1849 to 1901. He didn't grow up or live around here, as I understand it. He was from Illinois. His play, <u>Now and Then</u>, was his most well-known, and that's not saying much, because he only wrote one other play called <u>To Beat the Band</u>," Mrs. Portage said.

"If this is part of a play program, though, Mr. Beckett probably didn't have anything to do with it being put on around here—if it was put on around here at all," Katie felt a little downhearted at the fact that there was so little information on the piece of paper, and that it might all mean nothing.

"You're right, Katie. A lot of plays are put on long after the person that wrote them has died, but I don't think that that is necessarily the case here, dear, though I can't be certain," Mrs. Portage said. Katie saw that twinkle in Mrs. Portage's eyes again, and her spirits were lifted.

"I do remember that little old Beech Grove used to have an Opera House right here in town. I don't remember it myself because it was torn down before I was born. I remember my mother talking about what a wonderful part of the community it had been because it was the place where every event for miles would take place—pageants, shows, speakers, singers, dances, church revivals, you name it. I don't know why it was demolished, but I did learn from the man at the historical society that it had been built in 1898 and was torn down in 1929," Mrs. Portage revealed triumphantly.

"So it's possible that this play was put on at the Opera House in town somewhere between 1898 and 1929," Katie proclaimed. "Now we're getting somewhere!"

"Where was the Opera House at in town?" Katie asked with excitement.

"I knew that was the next thing you would ask!" Mrs. Portage said. "You're going to love this part! It was a very large building that stood right in the place where the Kimballs' and the Walshs' houses are today!"

"Oh wow!" Katie exclaimed. "And you didn't remember that it had been there, Mrs. P?"

"Well, dear. No. You see, I grew up on a farm outside of town. I didn't move to this house until I married my husband, Jack."

"Now the question is, why would an old, ripped off piece of a program be blowing around in my house for almost a hundred years?" Katie wondered if all this was leading somewhere or nowhere at all.

"I might have the answer to that, as well," Mrs. Portage winked.

"Mrs. Pimplepuff, you really are a detective! You really were 'on the case' all day while I was at school!" Katie nodded with approval.

"Well, it was either work on the Opera House mystery or clean out the front flower beds, and to tell you the truth, this was far more fun! It so happens that my brilliant detective mind had the sense to ask the man at the historical society what buildings were located around the Opera House during the time it was in use."

"And. . ." Katie couldn't quite see where Mrs. Portage was going with this.

"It just so happens that there was a small grocery store behind it on the next block. That was torn down about ten years before the Opera House because of a rat problem, but that is neither here nor there. The fascinating thing is that the house next to the Opera House was a boarding house where many of the actors that came to perform the plays stayed. It was owned by Mrs. Twilly. Many people that passed through town stayed at Mrs. Twilly's boarding house. Her rent was reasonable and she was a very good cook, that's what Mr. Luckring at the historical society told me," Mrs. Portage said matter of factly.

"Okay. . ." Katie said, still not able to fit this new piece into the puzzle.

"Think, little one. Whose house would that be?"

"Mine!" Katie shrieked loudly, jumping up from the table and knocking the leg of the table so hard that two cookies fell off of the mountain stacked on the plate in the center of the table.

"But my house can't still be the house that was the boarding house—that's way too long ago. I mean I know our house is old and all. . ." Katie trailed off.

"I think it is, dear. Do you have quite a few bedrooms upstairs?"

"Yeah," Katie said. "That's why Mom and Dad bought the house. Mom and Dad have their room, I have a room of my own and so does Neil. And there is a spare room piled with boxes for the catering business. Mom and Dad wanted lots of room because they weren't sure how many kids they wanted to have. Dad always said that the house was a good deal because it was a fixer-upper. He still works on repairing things when he has time. It is a big house, so it might be the original boarding house," Katie said, amazed.

"Most of the old houses around here do not have four bedrooms. So I'm sure it is the original boarding house. If actors

40

were staying at the boarding house, there were probably programs all over the place. That explains why the piece of the program would have been there. Heaven knows how it got stuck in the grate, though," Mrs. Portage said.

"I don't know how it got there, but I'm glad it did!" Katie smiled.

"I'm awfully glad it got stuck there, too, little one," Mrs. Portage said smiling back at Katie.

This was turning out to be the best afternoon that either of them had had in a very long time.

Chapter 9

Katie gently picked up the old yellowed piece of paper and looked at the front side a little longer. She was half afraid to turn it over because everything at this moment felt so exhilarating. This truly felt like it might be a real mystery. Maybe Katie's wish was coming true. But if she turned the paper over and found nothing of importance . . . well, then maybe it had just been a fun afternoon, mystery or not.

The fact that there was no year listed where the program said Saturday, October 23rd gave Katie some hope that even if the back side turned out to be nothing, at least she and Mrs. Portage could work on learning a little more about Beech Grove and what used to go on here. Maybe together they could trace the year that Now and Then was performed. It might make a good story for the local paper or even an interesting writing project for an English class in the future.

Katie had been staring at the paper, for a bit when her thoughts were interrupted by Mrs. Portage. "Katie, I did all the checking I could think to do about what was on the front side of the paper, but, as for whatever is on the back . . . I think that's a project for the two of us to do together. I tried to read it a couple of different times today, but I couldn't make it out. My eyes aren't what they used to be and I think it is time for a new prescription for my glasses."

"Mrs. P., did you try to read it right here at the table?" Katie asked.

"Yes, dear. Why?"

"I was just noticing that one of the light bulbs above your table is burned out. The light isn't very good in here to read by, I wouldn't think," Katie said, still not ready to turn the paper over yet—afraid that the excitement of the day was just about to end.

"I know. I have a devil of a time changing those things. You are probably right," Mrs. Portage sighed.

Sensing an opportunity to make the excitement last a little longer, Katie offered to change the light bulb for Mrs. Portage right then. Mrs. Portage eagerly accepted the offer and set off down the hall to the linen closet to find a spare bulb. Katie could hear Mrs. Portage mumbling the entire time about how awful it was to get old and not be able to do things like a youngster anymore.

While Katie waited for Mrs. Portage to come back, Katie took a long look around the kitchen. It reminded her of what she thought a grandmother's house should be. Katie didn't really know about a grandmother's kitchen from personal experience since Dad's parents had both died before Katie was born, and Mom's parents were what Mom herself called "nomads." Since they had retired, and that was a long time ago when Katie was just a kid, they traveled all around the country in an RV. About twice a year they ended up at the Trouts' to stay for a week or so. Katie loved them dearly, but she really couldn't say the kitchen on the inside of a motor home was a "granny" kind of kitchen. Katie suddenly realized that she had been living right down the street from Mrs. Portage her entire life and had never been in the kitchen before today.

It was a nice kitchen. Everything looked well cared for, but old. Mrs. Portage had small pots of plants on the windowsills. One pot was shaped like an odd-looking chicken. There were no dirty dishes in the sink, but a pile of clean ones were drying in a rack on the counter next to the sink. That made Katie notice that there was no dishwasher. Katie couldn't imagine her mom being able to survive without a dishwasher with all the cooking she did for Caterosities. But Katie supposed that if Mrs. Portage only cooked for herself, she really didn't need one.

The kitchen seemed like a really cozy room. That was the only word Katie could think of to describe it. The walls were yellow, like the color of a baby chick, and the curtains over the windows had blue and yellow flowers and all kinds of swirly green vines on them. None of the plants on the windowsill had brown on them and Katie found herself wondering if they were plastic. There was no way plants like that would survive at her house. Mom was great at many things, but keeping plants alive wasn't one of them.

Katie peeked at the refrigerator door. There were pictures stuck to it with magnets. The magnets all looked like different states. The Oregon magnet was holding a picture of three girls. One of them looked about Katie's age, and the other two looked younger. The Texas magnet was holding a picture of a smiling couple that was about her mom and dad's age, maybe a little younger. The Virginia and North Carolina magnets were attaching a large piece of orange construction paper with a finger painted picture of a rainbow with what Katie thought were two zebras under it.

Katie was still looking at the painting — and avoiding the piece of paper that she had laid on the table in front of her — when Mrs. Portage came back.

"Ta-dah! The little stinker was buried all the way behind the towels."

Mrs. Portage glanced where Katie was looking. "My great-granddaughter Kimberly made that for me. She's the littlest girl in the photo up there. She's five and is absolutely crazy about zebras."

Katie stood up and took the light bulb from Mrs. Portage, climbed on the kitchen chair and put her knee on the table to steady her balance. She had the old bulb out and the new one in in no time at all.

"I do wish I got to see them more than I do . . . My grandson, Eric, got married to a wonderful woman, and had those three girls, Alexia, Nicole, and Kimberly. The unfortunate thing is that he got offered a really great job and had to move to Texas. I only see them about twice a year. That's my other grandson, Connor, and his wife. They live in Florida. . ." Mrs. Portage's voice trailed off wistfully.

"I bet you miss them a lot," Katie said gently, as they both sat back down at the table.

"Yes, I do, little one. I get a bit lonely sometimes, but certainly not today!" Mrs. Portage said, grinning. "Now I think it's time to get down to the mystery of what is on the other side." Mrs. Portage reached into the pocket of her tan sweater and pulled out a large magnifying glass.

"Are you sure you didn't really read the writing already? The magnifying glass certainly would have helped you see the words," Katie said, looking at Mrs. Portage with raised eyebrows.

"Well, Katie, I did think about it, but I wanted to wait for you. Go on, give it a look see!"

Katie carefully turned over the paper and took the magnifying glass from Mrs. Portage. To give herself a few more seconds, she looked up instead of down to make certain that the light bulb she had changed was in proper working order. Mrs. Portage flipped the switch and the room lit up brightly. It was time to take a look.

Mrs. Portage's chair made a piercing squeal as she scooted it across the tile to be right next to Katie.

"Well. . ." Mrs. Portage said in an eager whisper.

The handwriting was scratchy and somewhat hard to read. It was even more difficult because it looked as if the words had been written in pencil and the writing had faded over time. As Katie put the magnifying glass over the words, she noticed that the paper was not flat, but wrinkly—as if it had been wet or crumpled up at one time. Katie bet that that was probably because the paper had been in her damp old house for what looked to be a pretty long time. It took Katie's eyes a moment to focus on the small scribbled words.

L.

Never mind what we said before—I just can't. I'll pick it up during the play. We might not have a chance to talk. Meet me at the train at 11:30 or if something seems wrong meet me at home where we found the big snapping turtle. Don't draw attention to yourself.

Love, B.

Chapter 10

Katie's heart was pounding so hard that she felt dizzy. She could actually hear her heartbeat in her ears. It was so loud that it drowned out Mrs. Portage's words, but that was all right, because all Mrs. Portage kept saying over and over was "Oh my! Isn't that something! Oh my!"

Katie reread the note to herself, and then Mrs. Portage asked her to read it again out loud. It was most certainly a mystery! Katie had so many questions racing through her head that it felt like the excitement and the questions added together were enough to completely make her head pop right off her body.

Mrs. Portage got up quickly headed straight for her desk. She rummaged through a stack of papers that had been neatly piled to grab a pad of paper and two pens. When she sat back down at the table, papers from the desk were completely disheveled and sliding to the floor, but Mrs. Portage didn't give them a second glance.

"Okay, little one. Here's what I want you to do. Read it again to me slowly, so that I can copy it down to study it. Then after that, together we'll come up with a list of questions that we need to find the answers to. Does that sound like a good idea?"

Katie could only nod her excitement. Even though she still felt dizzy, she did just as Mrs. Portage had said. When Mrs. Portage had recopied the note, she tore the top page off the pad and put it next to her, then handed the paper to Katie to make their list.

Together they formulated the questions that seemed most logical.

Who were L. and B.?

What couldn't be done?

What was going to be picked up?

Why might L. and B. be split up?

Where was the train?

Where was home?

Katie was amazed that one little note could leave so many unanswered questions! Just as Katie and Mrs. Portage were settling in to try to figure out some of the answers, the phone rang and startled both of them.

Mrs. Portage picked up the phone that had been sitting on the far side of the table, and answered it in a chipper voice.

"Hello...Oh, hi Andrea..." Katie looked up from the questions when she heard Mrs. Portage say her mother's name.

"Yes, she's here. We were just having a little chat. . ." Mrs. Portage looked at her watch. "Oh, certainly! I will send her right home. Thanks so much for letting her visit. I'd love it if she could come again!" Mrs. Portage winked at Katie, and Katie beamed her back a big smile.

As Mrs. Portage finished the call, Katie decided to make herself a quick copy of the note, as well. She thought it would be a good idea to keep the original in Mrs. Portage's lock box. As she jotted the words and Mrs. Portage hung up the phone, Katie asked, "What do you think this all means?"

"It means, Katie, that you and I are in for a bit of fun. But right now your mom needs you to get home to hop to your chores and homework. We have a lot to think on. That was a good idea making another copy of the note. Why don't you check with your parents to see if it would be okay if you came by again after school tomorrow? After we've read the note a few more times, maybe we'll figure out a starting point for our mystery."

Mrs. Portage said all this while she piled some of the cookies on a paper plate and slipped them into a big plastic zipper bag.

"I'm sure I'll be allowed to come back," Katie said excitedly.

"Katie, there is one other thing . . . I know this is exciting, to have a secret mystery, but I think it would be a good idea if you told your mom and dad about what you found."

"Okay, but why?" Katie asked.

"Well, your parents are two very intelligent people. And it would be good to know that we could turn to them if we need a little help. There is also the possibility that to solve this mystery we may need to do some research—like at the library and on the internet. You need to make certain that they are all right with the two of us doing this together, okay?" Mrs. Portage said this as she walked Katie to the door and handed her the plate of cookies. "Take these with you for you and your family. You were so excited that you didn't eat a single one while you were here!" Mrs. Portage laughed.

"Thank you, Mrs. Portage. Plan on me being here after school tomorrow!" Katie said as she trotted down the front steps and turned toward her house. She was delighted to have a new friend, and surprised that it wasn't the one she had expected it to be yesterday.

Chapter 11

Katie did just as Mrs. Portage had asked her. She talked to her parents about the note as soon as she got home. She had planned not to tell them everything — to keep a little bit of the mystery to herself, but she just couldn't. In all her excitement, she spilled the beans about everything — where she'd found the note, what the front said, what the back said — she didn't even have to pull her copy out of her backpack, because she had read it so many times already that she had it memorized. She told her parents about Mrs. Portage and what she had discovered on the internet and from the historical society about the Opera House, as well.

"And, did you know that our house was a boarding house where actors stayed in the early 1900's?" she asked her parents.

"Well, isn't that something!" Mr. Trout declared.

"It sounds like you and Mrs. Portage make a good team — look at all you've uncovered in just one day!" Mrs. Trout said smiling as she loaded crates with items to take to the women's meeting she was catering in an hour.

Katie thought that there would probably be no better time to ask than now. "Mom, Dad, would it be okay if Mrs. P. and I do some investigating together? You know, just going to the library, doing some checking on the internet, that sort of thing...she's really nice."

Mom and Dad glanced at each other, but didn't say a word to each other — they just smiled. Dad looked at Katie and said, "How about this . . . you are allowed to stop at Mrs. Portage's every day after school for an hour. If the two of you plan to go to the library or anywhere else, that's fine, we just need to know ahead of time, so we can make a plan. The other thing is this: you can work on this as long as your grades don't suffer. Deal?"

"Deal!" Katie agreed instantly.

"Now, do you want to come with us or go to the sitter's?" Mom asked.

For once, Katie actually wanted to go to the sitter's. Mrs. Buckridge had a study where it was quiet and Katie could do her homework. And tonight, unfortunately, she had a lot—math, some social studies, a spelling worksheet, and three chapters to read in <u>Frindle</u>. After all of that was done, she hoped she would have a little bit of time to work on deciphering the note.

Katie's homework didn't go nearly as quickly as she had hoped, and Mom and Dad were finished with catering sooner than usual, so Katie was back home, showered, and ready for bed by 9:30 p.m. She decided to hold off on reading the note or even letting herself think about it any more tonight. She knew that if she looked at her copy again, she would get herself all wound up and wouldn't be able to sleep. Besides that, she wanted to prove to Mom and Dad that she was responsible and able to make good choices. Going to bed before she was told could go a long way in keeping Mom and Dad happy.

Katie woke the next morning with a start. All she could remember as she tried to catch her breath was that she had been having a nightmare that a train was chasing her over a bridge and that she had had to jump into the water to save herself before the train hit her. In the dream, the train sank in the water, and Katie was working hard to stay afloat. The train had caused enormous waves and Katie was choking on the water as her head bobbed up and down. Suddenly there had been a hand that had reached out of a boat to grab Katie and pull her to safety. The hand was covered in powder and it left white marks on everything it touched. Katie knew that hand and thanked Mrs. Portage for saving her life, but Mrs. Portage was saying something . . . Katie couldn't quite hear her. . . It was coming out as a whisper . . . "Oh my . . . Isn't that something ? . . Oh my . . ."

Sometimes Katie had dreams that made absolutely no sense at all, but in this dream, Katie knew where at least some of the images had come from: the mystery note—the train, Mrs. Portage, and even what Mrs. Portage had been saying seemed related to the mystery. Katie couldn't wait to meet Mrs. P. after school. She would have to stop by her house this morning to tell her what Mom and Dad had said.

Katie hustled through her morning routine, kissed her parents and Neil and headed out the door. She knocked on Mrs. Portage's door, but there was no answer. Just as she turned to leave, a small folded piece of paper stuck in the doorjamb caught her eye. Katie didn't know if it was meant for her, but she had to check.

K.T.

I had to go get my hair done early this morning. I'll be watching for you after school. Hope you can make it! Have a great day!

Pimplepuff

P.S. I know about the train.

Katie smiled at the note, stuck it in her pocket, and headed to school. Once she was there, reality hit her again. Since the moment school had let out yesterday, she hadn't had one thought about Talia Blackwitt, but when Katie walked into the room, there she was, sitting at her desk that was still, unfortunately, next to Katie's. Katie decided that it was no big deal—yesterday had passed without a single problem. Maybe they would spend the rest of their school years politely ignoring each other. Katie wished hard for this as she sat down. Wishing hard just might make it happen.

Katie soon realized that Talia must have been so quiet yesterday because she had been plotting.

Ms Carone called the class to order, and told the students to start correcting the grammar sentences on the board. Katie pulled a pencil out of the stripy pencil case in her desk. The lead was broken completely off. She reached in and grabbed another; it was broken, too. Katie pulled all six pencils out and not a single one was usable without sharpening. That was weird. Katie took the handful of broken pencils up to the sharpener, sharpened them quickly and was back at her desk within a minute. As Katie put five of the pencils back in the case, she noticed that there were words written in marker in the bottom of the case. In big capital letters it simply said "I HATE YOU!" It startled Katie to see the words, and as she stared at them, she felt Talia staring at her.

Katie instantly thought that she should show this to Ms Carone, but then Talia would know she was upset, so Katie decided to ignore it. Even though she had stared at the words for a long time, Katie now popped her pencils in the case, zipped it up and started on the sentences as if nothing had happened.

At lunch, Katie went through the lunch line and headed over to sit by Tori and Jamie, two other nice fifth graders that were best friends, both of whom were very nice to Katie. As Katie walked past the end of the lunch table, though, she didn't see Talia stick her foot out. Katie didn't fall when she tripped, but she did drop her lunch tray.

It wasn't really a big deal—kids dropped lunch trays all the time; probably every person at the table had done it at least once since kindergarten, but this time was different. Instead of everyone just looking at Katie with looks that said, "It stinks when that happens," or "I'm glad it wasn't me this time," Talia piped up in a voice that sounded like she was talking to a baby, "Oohh! Did the little trout drop her fish food?" Everyone burst out laughing. It sounded like Talia was just making a joke, but Katie knew that she had tripped her and Katie could tell by the look in Talia's eyes that she was not joking at all.

Katie picked up her tray and the mess as best as she could, and then headed to the line to get another lunch. This time she was careful not to go past Talia.

The rest of the day was uneventful, but Katie knew that that was certainly not the end of Talia's nastiness. Katie decided that Talia was annoying and mean, but it wasn't worth talking to her parents about. There were some things she had to learn to take care of on her own. And dealing with Talia was one of them.

Chapter 12

Dealing with Talia's little nasty tricks made Katie all the more eager to get to Mrs. Portage's after school.

As soon as the last bell rang, Katie found herself running once again, to Mrs. Portage's house. Mrs. P. was standing on the front porch blowing on a steaming cup of tea in the chilly afternoon air.

"My my, little one, I don't believe I have ever seen you run to or from school before!" Mrs. Portage chuckled.

"Well,. . .I'm. . .not. . .a big fan. . .of running. . .anywhere!" Katie huffed.

"Yes, but we have business to tend to, don't we? Come in. I have a little surprise for you."

Katie sat right down at the kitchen table and dropped her backpack to the floor. She was relieved that it was empty except for her classroom copy of Frindle. She didn't have nearly as much homework as last night, just two more chapters to read.

Mrs. Portage handed Katie a tall glass of water and she gulped it right down. "This is for you, little one," Mrs. P. said as she placed a pink ballpoint pen and a small elastic-banded, polka-dotted notebook in front of Katie.

"What is this for?" Katie asked

"Every detective needs proper investigative tools to jot down facts and clues. I got a set for you and a set for me. What do you think?" Mrs. Portage asked as she wiggled her eyebrows up and down.

"I love them! Thank you so much," Katie said enthusiastically as she pulled the copy of the note out of her backpack and opened the notebook. "Your note this morning said that you know about the train, Mrs. P?"

"Yes! I got so excited about the note yesterday that I wasn't thinking clearly. The note specifically said, "*train at 11:30*" and last night I got to thinking-- I do remember when I was little, there used to be a train that ran right down Main Street. I can't tell you exactly when it was dismantled, but I do remember that you could buy tickets to ride it right where the Laundromat is now. There used to be a little window and a bell — it wasn't like a real station where you could sit down inside or anything. You just rang the bell and a little old man would open the window and sell you your ticket."

"Where did the train go?" Katie asked excitedly.

"I know it went from Beech Grove to Deerfield and on north to Rosewood, and even further. I don't think that it went south too terribly much further, though, but I could be mistaken."

"So that could mean that L. and B. were probably heading north, don't you think? But why would they need to leave so late at night? If they were actors, why wouldn't they go back to the boarding house after the play and leave the next morning?" Katie was confused.

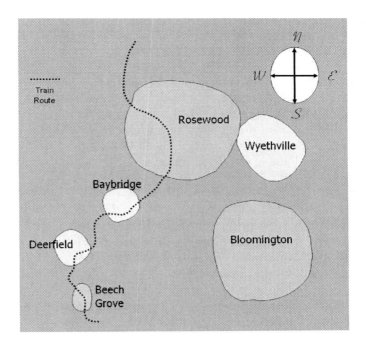

"I was thinking about that very thing all day today—at the beauty shop, at the grocery store, even when I went out to lunch with my good friend, Evelyn. Here's what I think—and I could be completely wrong, mind you!—maybe L. and B. were in trouble of some kind. Maybe they were criminals that were on the run. The train may have just been a meeting place before they left town or before or after they committed a crime. I don't know for sure if the train made stops that late at night, but it seems to me that it just might have if there were play performances that finished late in the evening. People that came to town by train to see the plays would have needed a way to get home. There was quite a bit of crime back then. But the same is true today, I suppose. It just seems to me that the note seems to be urgent," Mrs. Portage said in a rushed, excited whisper.

"That makes a lot of sense," Katie said. "The note also said, 'I'll pick it up during the play.' Maybe the IT in the note is something from a crime. Picking up something during a play seems like a time to do it when most people will be somewhere else. It sounds as if IT is pretty darn important—whatever it is! But if they were in the play, they couldn't really be committing a crime when they should be on stage—and if they were in a play, wouldn't people heading home on the train recognize them?"

"Whoa, there, little one. Catch your breath! I think we are getting ahead of ourselves. I'm thinking we need to do some research!" Mrs. Portage nodded. "Let's fire up the old computer to see if we can find out about actors between 1898-1929 that had initials L. or B. But before we do, I need to know if you talked to your mom and dad about all of this."

"I did. They said that it is absolutely fine. I think they are curious about what we'll discover. They didn't know that our house had been a boarding house. Dad just said that I need to tell him if we'll be going anywhere to do research before we go and that I can be here for an hour everyday after school, and I have to make sure to keep my grades up."

"I don't expect that that will be a problem for you, little one!" Mrs. Portage said in a way that made Katie feel like she was the smartest fifth grader that had ever been.

As Katie moved a kitchen chair over to Mrs. Portage's desk, she noticed that Mrs. Portage had picked up and organized all of the papers that she had disarranged yesterday when she was looking for a pad of paper. Everything was once again in neat, orderly piles. Mrs. Portage sat down in the chair that wasn't directly in front of the computer, and motioned for Katie to sit down to do the typing. While they waited for Mrs. Portage's computer to start up, Mrs. Portage asked Katie how school had been today.

Katie looked away from Mrs. Portage. She didn't want to tell Mrs. P. about Talia any more than she wanted to tell her parents. But Katie didn't feel right about not telling her anything at all. They were friends; maybe Mrs. Portage would have some advice. Without making it sound like she was upset by the situation, Katie told Mrs. Portage about Talia's first day at school—that they had been paired up, but that Talia was mad at Katie because Katie's dad had quit Talia's father's business and that Talia's family had had to move, and that Talia blamed Katie. She told Mrs. P. about the broken pencils, the "I hate you" in the pencil case, and how Talia had tripped her and made fun of her at lunch today.

Mrs. Portage's mouth was pinched tightly shut, as if she had to lock her lips together to keep from exploding on Katie's behalf. After a few moments, Mrs. Portage calmed herself down enough to ask Katie if her parents knew what was going on.

"Yes—most of it. I told them what had happened Monday, and they are more than willing to help me, but I don't think I'll tell them about the whole lunch thing today. I don't want to worry them."

"That is sweet of you, dear, but that's what parents do best— worry—you can't take that job away from them by not telling them what happened. That won't stop their worrying."

"I know," Katie said. "I just think, for a while anyway, I want to handle it on my own."

Mrs. Portage looked at Katie very seriously before she spoke. "I guess that I can understand that, but you need to make certain that you talk to them if this Talia gets to be too much to handle. Remember, I'm always here to talk to, as well. You just say the word, and I can make things happen. I may look like a scrawny little old lady that could blow over in a hard wind, but I bet you didn't know that I have a black belt in Tae Kwon Do. I can see to it that this Talia stops messing with you. Having a granny show up to take her down at recess might just knock her down a peg or two! Of course, I'm counting on you cracking open the old piggy bank to bail me out of jail, if that happens!" Katie couldn't believe that Mrs. Portage was able to make her laugh so easily about the Talia fiasco.

Finally the computer was ready, and an exhaustive search of everything they could think of related to the Beech Grove Opera House, the play Now and Then, and actors that performed in Beech Grove, specifically ones with the initials L. or B., led absolutely nowhere.

"I can tell by the look on your face, little one, that you're disappointed. I must admit, I am too. But you have to remember, not all mysteries are solved in just a few short days. Some take months, even years, to solve. We have to be patient and not lose hope, and above all, think logically. So, let's walk through what we know. I found about everything there was to find on the internet about the playwright, Thurgood Beckett, who wrote Now and Then yesterday—and that wasn't much. I don't think that Beckett really has anything to do with our mystery since he was only the writer of the play, and I found no evidence that he had ever even been to Beech Grove," Mrs. Portage said matter-of-factly.

Katie nodded quietly. "Maybe we would have more luck finding out about all of this if we went to the historical society. It's more likely that they would have information about Beech Grove and what went on here. I don't think that the history of our little town has made its way to cyberspace yet."

"I'll bet you're right, Katie. But I bet there might be a whole lot of information stuffed into some dusty old filing cabinets only one town away. The Lindeman County Historical Society is in Deerfield and it houses all kinds of records, pictures, and articles for the entire county. We don't have enough time to go today, but if we head there right after school, I'll bet we'd have enough time to do a little research tomorrow."

Katie nodded eagerly.

"You need to ask your parents if going to Deerfield tomorrow would be all right and if maybe you could have permission to stay with me until about 5:30. We could do our research and grab a bite to eat, as well. Do you think they'll go for it?" Mrs. Portage asked.

Katie was certain they would.

Chapter 13

When Katie got home, she filled Mom and Dad in on how the Opera House mystery investigation was going. She also swore them to complete secrecy. Even though Mrs. Portage and Katie hadn't discovered much yet, Katie was really beginning to feel that they were on to something. Katie got permission from her mom to go with Mrs. Portage to the historical society in Deerfield the next afternoon and to the Deerfield Public Library, too, if they needed to find out more information. Katie's dad even agreed to give her money to go out to eat with Mrs. Portage. Katie just had to make certain she was home by 7:00 and that she would be able to take care of her chores and her homework.

When Katie's parents asked her how school had been and if Talia had been any trouble, she told them honestly that Talia had been a bit mean, but that she wanted to try to take care of it herself for a while. Katie's parents made her promise that if Talia became too much, she would tell them immediately. Katie swore that she would.

After Katie's homework and chores were completed, she got Dad's approval to do some searching on the internet. As she sat and stared at the blank rectangle where she wanted to type in a search criteria, she realized that she didn't quite know what she wanted to search for. She had a gnawing feeling that she was overlooking something simple.

Katie asked herself what a real detective would do. She knew immediately: go back to the evidence.

Katie pulled her notebook and her handwritten copy of the note out of her backpack and stared at it. She didn't know where to begin. Katie absentmindedly twirled the paper between her fingers and accidentally the small piece of notebook paper fluttered to the floor. As Katie bent over to pick it up, she stopped and stared at it for a moment. It hadn't landed on the side where she had copied the words from the note. It had landed so that the blank side was up. She suddenly realized that she hadn't bothered to copy down the information about the play that had been on the other side. It was not a problem—she had that memorized.

...presents <u>Now and Then</u> a play by Thurgood Beckett

Saturday, October 23rd

Katie suddenly realized that even though the internet hadn't provided any information about the Beech Grove Opera House, and had provided very little about Thurgood Beckett, there was something that she could find out right now. With just a few keystrokes and clicks of the mouse, Katie suddenly found what just a few minutes ago she hadn't even known she would be searching for—the possible years the play had been performed.

Katie knew that the year had to be between 1898 and 1929 since that was the time that the Opera House was in use in Beech Grove. Katie also knew that days of the week didn't always fall on the same date—like her birthday—it had been on a Wednesday last year and a Thursday this year, but her next birthday would be on a Saturday. Katie used these facts, and typed "calendar 1898" into the search area. Right away a website came up that she knew would help. At the site, a person could find out the date of any day in any year. She clicked on it and was able to see that October 23rd did not fall on a Saturday that year. Katie took her time and checked every year through 1929.

Even though Katie's search wasn't exact, she was thrilled with what she found. Instead of having 31 possible years to find information about, Katie had found that October 23rd had only fallen on a Saturday four different years: 1909, 1915, 1920, and 1926.

Katie wanted to call Mrs. Portage and tell her about her discovery, but decided that it would make a nice surprise tomorrow.

The next morning, Mrs. Portage was standing on her porch in a big fluffy blue bathrobe with matching slippers and her hair wrapped up in a scarf with butterflies all over it. She was sipping another cup of tea.

"Today is no problem with Mom and Dad," Katie said at the bottom of the steps, bending down, trying to catch her breath. "I'm allowed to stay until 7:00 p.m. and they gave me money for my dinner!" Katie thought about telling Mrs. Portage about her discovery about the four possible years of the play, but decided to wait until later.

"Stupendous! I'll meet you here. You'd better get a move on, little one. And remember. . ."

Katie turned around to look at Mrs. Portage, and found her posing in an absurd position for an old lady: her one hand held her teacup and the other one was a tight little fist held up in front of her chest. Mrs. P. looked like she was getting ready to attack — to either punch someone or possibly douse an enemy with hot chamomile tea. Just then she threw her right leg out in front of her and made a huge screech that made Katie think of a huge bird attacking, "Yeeeeeaaahhh!" The kick that she gave the air in front of her was seriously enough to knock over any fifth or even sixth grader. Katie was both startled and amazed — Mrs. Portage hadn't even spilled a drop of tea.

"You were really serious about the black belt?" Katie asked as she headed down the block.

"I'm as serious as a heart attack, little one! Of course, it has been a few years," Mrs. Portage grinned, her eyebrows wiggling up and down.

Katie's day was less eventful with Talia than the day before had been. When Katie had gotten up to get a Kleenex, Talia had shoved Katie's math book off of her desk and onto the floor. But it didn't have the effect that Talia had been hoping for, Katie was sure. Since Talia had done it quickly, so she wouldn't be caught, she had misjudged and done it too forcefully. The math book had hit Hunter Thorne in the back. He had turned around to yell at Katie, but Katie was still at the wastebasket throwing her tissue away. "Knock it off!" he had said in a mean voice to everyone in the vicinity since he couldn't figure out who the actual culprit was. He picked the book up off the floor, tossed it back on Katie's desk, and turned back around. No one had seen what had actually happened, but Katie knew.

Nothing but mean stares from Talia to Katie occurred the rest of the day, but every time Katie looked up to stare back at Talia, Talia looked away. Katie realized after about the fifth dirty look, that maybe Talia wasn't as tough as she pretended to be. She couldn't even look Katie straight in the eye. This alone made Katie feel a great deal braver.

When school finally ended, Katie was grateful that for the second night in a row she didn't have much homework. This was fantastic, because she and Mrs. Portage had a lot to do.

When Katie reached Mrs. Portage's house, she saw Mrs. P.'s green car sitting out on the street. Katie didn't look inside, and as she turned to head up the steps to the porch, she heard the horn blare twice. Katie turned toward the car and saw Mrs. Portage leaning across the seat and waving to her from behind the steering wheel through the passenger window.

Katie threw her backpack into the backseat, climbed in the front and buckled her seat belt. "Wow! Talk about being ready to go!" Katie said amazed.

"Little one, time's a wastin'! We've got to hustle!" Mrs. Portage replied as she put the car in gear.

They reached the Lindeman County Historical Society in Deerfield in less than seven minutes. Katie was a little surprised by the way Mrs. Portage drove. She knew that some older people were not exactly speedy when it came to driving, but Mrs. P. could certainly hold her own on the roads.

With matching notebooks and pens in hand, they headed in to see Mr. Luckring—the man that had answered Mrs.Portage's questions about the Opera House on Tuesday. Katie almost giggled out loud when she suddenly recalled that Mrs. Portage had identified herself as Mrs. Pimplepuff to this man two days ago. Katie made sure to refer to Mrs. P. by her code name when they were talking.

Mr. Luckring was a tall, older gentleman with a white beard and not a single hair on his head. The beard was scruffy and long—way too long, Katie thought. It looked to her like he was growing as much hair as he could from his chin to make up for the fact that there was none on the top of his head. He nodded hello to them as they walked in the door, and went back to cleaning the glass on the front of the big display cabinet that had a really old dingy baseball uniform that said "Beech Grove Pirates" on it, and a shelf full of framed black and white photographs of baseball teams wearing the same exact uniforms.

Katie noticed that the room smelled like glass cleaner, but something else, as well. Even though the big case was closed tightly, Katie thought the other smell was the uniform—a dusty, musty moist basement kind of smell. Maybe it wasn't the uniform—it might have been all the years of memories that were piled up in the room. The display case was in the center of the room and it was spotless. The rest of the room, however, looked like someone was in the process of either moving in or moving out. There were old, dented cardboard boxes piled against one wall in stacks that were taller than Katie. There was a long table against the back wall with papers strewn about, and behind the table were sixteen mismatched filing cabinets of different sizes.

"Are you moving the historical society somewhere else?" Katie asked Mr. Luckring.

"Certainly not!" he replied in a raspy, tired voice. "What would make you think that?"

"Oh, I'm sorry. I saw all the boxes piled up over there. I just thought. . ." Katie spoke a little embarrassed.

"No, no," Mr. Luckring said a bit more gently. "That's just stuff that people drop off because they want to get rid of it and they think it might be stuff important for someone around here to hang on to. But we don't have enough room to put out every trophy that anyone in this county ever got for whatever it was they happened to do. We just don't have any place to store the stuff. Can I help you ladies with something?"

Mrs. Portage spoke up and said, "Why, yes, we are certainly hoping so. My young friend here is doing a report for school on the Beech Grove Opera House, and we were wondering if you might be able to help us with finding some information on a play that had been performed there."

Mr. Luckring looked at Mrs. Portage and shook his head slowly as if she had just asked him if he wouldn't mind helping the two of them move the Empire State Building to downtown Beech Grove.

"You're the woman that called the other day—Pimplepuff, wasn't it? Unusual name. Look lady, I appreciate your attempts to help this girl with her education, but like I told you the other day, the Opera House was around from 1898 to 1929—that's over thirty years of papers to rummage through. Unless you have the name of the play and the year it was performed, a search like that could take me days."

"We do have the name of the play!" Mrs. Portage said hopefully.

"It's a start, but it'll still take quite a while," Mr. Luckring said, shaking his head again.

"Would it help if I could give you only four years to search in?" Katie asked hesitantly.

"Help? Honey, that would take your search down to about an hour and a half, give or take," Mr. Luckring said with a huge smile of relief.

Mrs. Portage stared at Katie with a look of utter amazement as Katie opened her notebook and showed Mr. Luckring the four years—1909, 1915, 1920 and 1926. As Mr. Luckring squinted at file cabinet drawers, Katie whispered to Mrs. Portage about her internet search last night, and how simple it had been to narrow down the years.

In another minute, Mr. Luckring said, "Here's what we'll do—there are three of us and four years to search. Each file drawer contains a couple of years of information about things that happened then. The years are marked on the front, see? None of it is organized very well within the drawers. What say we each take a year and start searching? If we don't find what you're looking for, I'll look through the fourth year tomorrow and let you know. What are we searching for anyway?"

"Anything about a play called <u>Now and Then</u> by Thurgood Beckett. We know that it was performed on Saturday, October

23rd of one of those four years," Mrs. Portage said beaming at Katie.

"It's not a whole heck of a lot, but it's a start. I'll take 1909. You ladies pick a year and start searching. Don't get stuff all messed up in the drawers—not any worse than it already is, anyway."

For the next hour barely a word was spoken between Mrs. Portage, Katie and Mr. Luckring. Mr. Luckring every once in a while would make a grunt when he found something interesting—something that he had to make an effort to remember where it had been found for future reference. Occasionally, Mr. Luckring would let out a raspy cough like the musty surroundings that he worked in were taking a toll on his lungs, but other than that—not a word.

Katie hoped it would be she who found whatever it was that they were looking for—an article about the play, a small poster that might have hung somewhere in public to announce the play, anything, but even if she couldn't be the one to make the discovery, she just hoped there was a discovery of something to be made.

Suddenly, Mrs. Portage let out a gasp, "Well, looky there!" She passed what she had found to Katie. It was an exact replica of the torn piece of the program that Katie had found in her heating grate—only this one was full-size. It was almost the size of a regular 8 ½ x 11" piece of paper and it was neatly folded in half.

Just as Katie had had a hard time turning over the original piece of paper because she had been anxious about what she would find, she was now having a hard time opening the folded sheet because the anticipation of what it might say inside was more than she could handle. Katie felt as if she had just gotten a shocking zap of electricity.

She heard Mrs. Portage rifling through her drawer again to check if there happened to be anything else related to the play as she talked to Mr. Luckring. Katie heard their brief conversation, but it was as if it was from a huge distance.

". . . I think we've found exactly what we were looking for. Is there a way to make a copy of this?"

"Yes, indeed. Copy machine is right over there. That didn't take nearly as long as I expected. Just out of curiosity, what drawer was it in?"

"1920," Mrs. Portage said as she slipped the folded paper out of Katie's hand, unfolded it, made a copy of both sides of the sheet, and thanked Mr. Luckring for all of his help.

Chapter 14

Katie hadn't been able to say a word as they left the historical society, and Mrs. Portage didn't seem to mind thanking Mr. Luckring and wishing him a good evening.

Once they were back in the car, Katie breathlessly said, "I couldn't bring myself to look at the inside. Did you look at it when you made the copy?"

"Nope. I closed my eyes—I guess I was too excited, and wanted to wait until we were by ourselves. Tell you what, why don't we grab a bite to eat and take a look at the program? Do you want fast food or a sit down restaurant?"

"Well, I'd love to go in and sit down to eat, but I'm afraid someone might overhear us talking. Could we maybe, get fast food and eat in the car?" Katie could tell by looking at the inside of Mrs. Portage's car that she wasn't persnickety about eating and drinking in her car. There was a granola bar wrapper on the seat between them and a big empty Styrofoam cup in the cup holder.

"I like your thinking, little one!" Mrs. Portage nodded. They headed to the only fast food restaurant in Deerfield, on the corner of Vine Avenue and Church Street; then, since it was only ten minutes after five, they went to Firefly Park to eat and watch the little kids play in the crisp October late afternoon.

Katie was both famished and eager to talk about what they had found not ten minutes before. Katie started munching her fries as Mrs. Portage pulled out the two photocopied pages from her notebook. Katie saw that the top one was the front side of the program. Part of it looked exactly like the piece of paper in the lockbox, only with the year 1920 under "Saturday, October 23rd." Above the word 'presents' in large loopy letters the program said "The Beech Grove Theatrical Association proudly'. The other half of the 8 ½ x 11" page, the part that would have been the back cover when it was folded in half, was blank. The page underneath, though, was a mystery. Mrs. Portage put the papers on the seat in between them. The one that they hoped contained at least one clue, and maybe more, was hidden on the bottom.

"Okay, Katie, let's take a minute to catch our breath and eat our sandwiches. Then we can see what's on the other paper. Let's not eat so fast that we choke, though," Mrs. Portage said as she began stuffing huge bites of cheeseburger into her mouth. Katie nodded agreement as she sucked her milkshake straw with such force that she thought her eyes might pop out of their sockets.

In minutes they had finished and were wiping their greasy fingers on paper napkins. Mrs. Portage slowly removed the top page from the seat, revealing the page that they hadn't seen before.

Mrs. Portage and Katie were quiet as they stared at the copy of the inside of the program. On the left side of the full sized page there was nothing, but on the right side, at the top were a few sentences that summarized the play:

"Now and Then is the dramatic story of two sisters who love the same man. Sisters who, despite their growing hatred of one another, find that family ties must prevail, even though the cost may seem almost too much to bear."

The middle of the program page contained a brief paragraph about the playwright, Thrugood Beckett. On the bottom half of the right side in small print was the name of the director, John Howell, and a list of other plays he had directed. Under that information was the cast list. The information that was inside the program was shorter than Katie expected, and she felt a bit dejected when she noticed that there was absolutely no information given about any of the actors other than their names.

Matthew Carbuncle .... played by Thomas Madden
Cornelia Sankroft .... played by Virginia Kellogg
Prudence Sankroft .... played by Olivia Dixon
Franklin Harlow .... played by William Tate

"Katie, there's got to be a clue right here in front of us," Mrs. Portage said matter-of-factly, but the longer they stared at every word on the page, the harder it was to find anything that remotely resembled a clue.

"Well," Mrs. Portage said after what seemed like an eternity of staring at words, "at least we have a list of names now—four cast members and the director."

"Yes, but none of them have the initial L. or B."

"But at least we have the next step down the path. We still have time. Let's head over to the library and see what information we can dig up on any of these people." Mrs. Portage sounded upbeat about the chance that they could maybe find another clue before their time today was up.

As Mrs. Portage drove, Katie read the mysterious note out loud to refresh them both on the details since Katie didn't want to have to get the note out in the library for fear of someone seeing it.

L. Never mind what we said before — I just can't. I'll pick it up during the play. We might not have a chance to talk. Meet me at the train at 11:30 or if something seems wrong meet me at home where we found the big snapping turtle. Don't draw attention to yourself. Love, B.

At the library, Mrs. Portage sat at one computer and Katie perched herself at the computer right next to her. They had agreed on the way into the library that Katie would see what she could find out about any of the people in the program. Since they now had a year—1920—and Katie and Mrs. Portage still suspected that whoever wrote the note was somehow involved in some sort of crime, (the secret "it" in the note, made that a pretty safe hunch, they both thought), Mrs. Portage would check out crimes around Beech Grove in the year 1920 to see if any of the names on the list popped up.

By 6:30 p.m. Katie had found some information, but she didn't know if one ounce of it was relevant to the Opera House mystery. Katie found the obituary for John Howell, the director, in the archives of the old Weekly Commercial—the local paper that was no longer in print. The obituary said that he had died in 1941 after a long illness. Mr. Howell had been a school teacher and had been married for 22 years. The obituary said that he adored his wife and children and had loved teaching, reading, volunteering at church and donating his time to the Opera House when it was the community focal point. The obituary quoted Mr. Howell as saying that he loved the Opera House and the Theatrical Association because they had "allowed me the chance to meet such interesting people from all over the United States right in my own backyard."

After picking a random name from the list, Katie also found out that Virginia Kellogg was from New York City. In 1932 she won an award for her small, but meaningful role in a movie that Katie had never heard of. The article that Katie found on Miss Kellogg simply stated that "before moving to New York, Virginia had paid her dues by traveling around the country performing in small town theaters. It is astounding that a single girl could provide for herself on such meager pay. Miss Kellogg was the epitome of the 'starving artist.'" The article also stated that she died in 1954 in an automobile accident.

Katie found absolutely nothing about a Thomas Madden who would have been living in 1920. By the time she had finished a search on him, Mrs. Portage had finished checking on crimes in the Deerfield/Beech Grove area around the same time. She had come up empty. All of the crimes had been small in nature — someone stealing gasoline from the local station, a rampage of small fires being set to abandoned barns by a bunch of hoodlums, a grocery store break-in, and other smaller crimes — none of which involved a single name from the program.

Katie said, "Since I don't have much homework, I think I'll be allowed to search some more tonight for information about the two names on the list that I didn't get to: Olivia Dixon and William Tate."

Katie and Mrs. Portage walked out into the brisk evening air to the car at a quick pace. It was already 6:45 p.m. and it was almost a ten minute drive home. Katie was expected home by 7:00.

As they reached the car, Mrs. Portage stopped short, and pulled the program copy out of her notebook. Katie hopped into the car and waited for Mrs. Portage, but she just stood outside the driver's door for another long moment looking at the program.

Katie reached across the seat and opened the door. "Mrs. P., I don't mean to rush you, but we need to get a move on, so that I'm not late getting home. I want to make sure that I do everything I'm supposed to so that we can keep working on this," Katie said in a kind, but rushed tone.

"Oh, sorry dear, but I think I just realized something," Mrs. Portage said slipping into the car, starting the ignition, and handing Katie the page.

"What?" Katie said, feeling a small pang of excitement.

"Katie, I think there is another clue right here in front of us. Take a closer look at the cast of the play."

Katie did as Mrs. Portage said, but if the clue that Mrs. Portage was talking about was right here in plain sight, Katie felt like she might as well be blind. She was missing it.

"Mrs. Portage, I don't see the clue. Can you show me?" Katie asked, feeling like she wasn't quite as keen a detective as she had believed herself to be.

"I think you should study it a bit longer—look at the two names that you didn't have a chance to find information on yet. We are two very intelligent women, and if we come to the same conclusion about those names, we'll know we're on the right track." Mrs. Portage backed out of the library parking lot and drove quietly back toward Beech Grove so that Katie could have some time to think.

Katie was perplexed for a few moments. Olivia Dixon and William Tate—the names had nothing in common. Way back then, Katie figured that most women who got married changed their last name to their husband's. Since the last names didn't match, Katie thought it was a pretty safe bet that they weren't married to each other. But that, alone, certainly wasn't much of a clue. Picking two names off of a page and saying, "Yep, I'm pretty sure they're not married" didn't mean much of anything.

Katie tried to keep from getting frustrated, and it paid off. After only a couple of minutes, the clue that Mrs. Portage had mentioned jumped off the page so fast that Katie actually felt lightheaded. "Mrs. Portage, my full name is Katelyn, but everyone calls me Katie. Is there that kind of nickname for Olivia?"

"Ah, yes, my dear, there certainly is—it's Liv, sometimes Livy!"

"And a lot of times guys named William are called Bill or Billy, aren't they?"

"Yes, indeed, my little one! You got it!"

Chapter 15

"It was right there in plain sight! We spent all of that time in the library and staring at the page, and there it was screaming at us!" Katie practically yelled.

"Hold on there, little one. It's a possibility that Olivia Dixon was called Livy and that William Tate was Billy, but we don't know that for sure. It may be some great coincidence that we are looking for names that start with L and B, and these two *may* have had nicknames that began with those letters. We can't be sure. We have to think logically about this." Mrs. Portage said all of this in a calm, logical way, but Katie noticed that she hadn't quit smiling or lost the twinkle in her eye.

"You're right, Mrs. P. We can't hang our hopes on this one clue — or coincidence. We have to keep searching. I'm so excited I can't stand it! I hope Mom and Dad will let me do a little more research tonight," Katie said breathlessly.

As Mrs. Portage pulled up in front of the Katie's house, Katie saw the little green digital numbers on Mrs. Portage's dashboard clock flick to 6:56 p.m. Katie gave a sigh of relief as she pointed to the clock.

Mrs. Portage gave her a smile and a quick hug. "I'll do a little internet search of my own tonight. Being a little old lady that lives by herself, I have the advantage of staying up as late as I want. So even if you don't have time to research, I will. See you after school tomorrow?" Mrs. Portage asked eagerly.

Katie could tell by her expression that Mrs. Portage didn't just want to get together to work on solving the mystery. She genuinely liked spending time with Katie. That fact alone made Katie feel terrific. Katie hopped out of the car, grabbed her backpack from the back seat, gave Mrs. Portage a wave and a nod and dashed to the door.

Katie was surprised to see her parents sitting on the couch together, Mom with her head on Dad's shoulder, when she walked in. Neil had drug the huge box of building blocks out of the closet and had built a doghouse for Diamond. Mom and Dad were both laughing as they watched Neil try to nudge Diamond into the house. As Diamond turned around, one side of the building collapsed, and Neil scurried to rebuild it. While he did that, Diamond quietly slunk out of the doghouse and tried to hide where Neil couldn't find him, but as soon as the fallen wall was rebuilt, the two-year-old was searching behind and under all the furniture looking for the patient dog, and the process started all over again.

"They've been doing this for half an hour," Dad said chuckling. "That dog is a darn good sport to put up with it! Hey, kiddo, how'd you make out on your detectivating today? Hey is that a real word?"

"If it isn't, it should be. And it went great! We might have found another clue!"

Mom sat up eagerly. "Well, are you going to tell us?"

"Mrs. Portage and I aren't sure if it is anything yet. Give me a little more time to check it out first."

"Fair enough," Mom said, but she looked slightly disappointed. "Hey, how is it going with Talia?"

"Not horrible," Katie said honestly, since today had been fairly uneventful—only the math book incident had occurred and it hadn't been a big deal.

"'Not horrible' doesn't mean the same thing as 'pretty good.' Are you sure you're okay?" Dad asked gently.

"I'm fine--really! It's nice to see the two of you actually sitting down together. Why do you have the night off, anyway, Mom?" Katie wondered.

"Apparently, everyone in the community is either cooking for themselves tonight or going out to dinner. We had nothing on the calendar for tonight. Isn't it wonderful? Hey, and guess what! Nothing is scheduled for tomorrow, either. I was thinking that since it's unusual to have a Friday night off, we really need to do something special together. Ideas?"

Katie was eager to spend time together, just the four of them—especially since it didn't happen all that frequently, but she was a little torn between doing something as a family and spending time with Mrs. Portage.

Mom must have seen what Katie was thinking, because before she could say a word, Mom continued, "How about this? Tomorrow evening we go to the museum in Bloomington. Remember, I catered the grand opening about two months ago? They have all kinds of neat exhibits. I had wanted to take some time to look at things when I was there, but the place was packed. The one exhibit is on North American birds, and one is some artist's paintings, and there are a few other exhibits, too, but I can't for the life of me remember on what. Anyway, if we do that tomorrow night, then you would have some extra time to spend with Mrs. Portage, if you wanted, on Saturday."

Dad was nodding as if the whole thing sounded like a wonderful idea, even though spending a whole evening in the Bloomington Museum was not at the top of Dad's "ooh, that sounds exciting list," Katie was sure. Nor was it at the top of hers. But they would all be together, and that would be nice. Katie readily agreed.

Mom told Katie that she couldn't go to Mrs. Portage's after school tomorrow. She needed to get home and get changed so that they could leave quickly. The museum was open until nine o'clock, but since this was going to be an outing, Dad said that they might as well go out to dinner first. Mom jumped at the chance to have someone else do the cooking.

Katie excused herself to call Mrs. Portage to let her know of the change in plans. She found her phone number in the little directory that Mom kept by the phone. Katie took a second to memorize it. Since they were working together, Katie thought it might be a good idea to commit her number to memory.

Katie could tell that Mrs. Portage was trying to hide the fact that she was slightly disappointed from Katie. "Oh, it's quite all right, little one. You can come over anytime you'd like on Saturday. Come to the back. I might be outside doing some yard work. If I'm not, you just come right in the back door and give a holler. Hey, I just thought of something. Hold on just a minute. . ." Katie heard Mrs. Portage plop down the receiver and start shuffling papers. She began talking again before she had even picked up the phone.

"Oh, my goodness, Katie. You are not going to believe this, but you just might be able to do some detective work tomorrow night after all," Mrs. Portage exclaimed.

"I'm afraid not, Mrs. P. We're leaving pretty early—almost right after school, and I don't have any idea what time we'll be home," Katie said apologetically.

"No, dear. I mean while you're out. Didn't you say that you are going to the Bloomington Museum?"

"Yes, but what does that have to do with our case?"

"Maybe nothing at all, but I got a flier in the mail a couple of weeks ago for the Bloomington Museum—I just dug it out from the pile of papers on my desk. It says here that there are five exhibits. They all look quite interesting, but the one in particular, might be especially worth your time: 'Infamous Crimes and Criminals—A Look into Ohio's Unsavory Notables.' I had been meaning to take my friend Evelyn to the museum to see the 'North American Birds—Fascinating Flights' exhibit, but I hadn't had a chance. I remembered seeing the flier and thinking to myself that the exhibit on criminals seemed a little peculiar. Little did I know that that would be one of such interest to me only a few weeks later. Don't go expecting to find something big, dear. It may be nothing. Right now, we don't know what kind of crime we're dealing with, or even if there is a crime at all. It's just a shot in the dark. However, logical minds use every opportunity to gather facts. Don't forget to take your notebook, Katie."

Katie agreed. As they said goodbye, Mrs. Portage assured Katie that she would do a thorough search on Olivia Dixon and William Tate, and that was a good thing since Katie had the growing feeling that she might not be able to tonight. She still had to read a little of <u>Frindle</u> for homework, get a shower, and fold a laundry basket full of socks and underwear that Mom had subtly placed on Katie's favorite blue living room chair. In addition to that, Katie was feeling pretty worn out—probably from all the excitement of the day.

Katie decided that holding off on doing any more research tonight wasn't such a bad thing. She decided to shower quickly and do her reading right before bed. Katie could match the stupid socks while spending a little time with her family. She could hear Neil and her parents giggling in the living room and the sounds of one of her favorite old black and white movies starting. As Katie put the phone back in the charger, she knew she smelled popcorn.

The mystery had waited close to one hundred years; it could wait one more night.

Chapter 16

Katie was dressed and eating her breakfast before her alarm would usually have gone off. She was really looking forward to the day. Katie had a nugget of hopefulness about finding another clue tonight at the Bloomington Museum, but she had enough sense not to let it get out of hand. She didn't want to spend too much time thinking about it, because there was a chance—more like a huge likelihood, in fact, that nothing would come of the outing except a nice time out with Mom, Dad and Neil.

Katie had awoken with an idea and wanted to get to school early. Last night, as she was falling asleep, Katie had been glad that she had spent time with her family watching the movie and munching popcorn, but she had realized that she wouldn't have time after school to do her own search on Olivia Dixon and William Tate since Mom had said they needed to leave pretty much right after school. Katie also knew Mom, and it didn't matter how early Katie got up--there was no way she would be allowed on the computer before school. Katie also knew that Mom was right with that rule since Katie had a huge tendency to lose track of time whenever she got involved in something like a good book or an internet search. That was why it was so important that Katie got to school before the first bell to talk to Mr. McKeever, her math, science and computer teacher.

Katie was certain that Mrs. Portage would do, or maybe had already done, a big search on the two actors, but Katie really liked the search as much as she liked what she hoped was a great solution to the mystery. Katie also felt the need to prove herself—not to Mrs. Portage—but to herself. Katie knew it didn't matter to Mrs. Portage which of them found what clue since they were in this together. That part didn't really matter to Katie, either. What mattered was the idea of knowing she was capable of doing something big--that she wasn't just an ordinary kid—or maybe that she was just an ordinary kid, but that she could make a difference.

Katie was tired of always being overlooked by kids her own age. She knew that most of them thought of her as "the nice girl that's pretty smart, but can't play sports very well," and that was it — well, other than them thinking "what a bummer to have a last name that's a fish." She knew that most of the kids in her class thought she was all right (except for Talia, of course), but the problem was she didn't make much of an impression. Katie sighed to herself, thinking that she supposed that it was better to make no impression than a bad impression.

The funny thing was that Katie saw her life divided into two different boxes. In the box with her family and now Mrs. Portage, she knew she was special. In the other box with all of her classmates Katie felt, well, whatever the absolute flip-side of special was. Katie knew in her heart that the opinions in the second box didn't really matter, but that didn't stop her wanting to make the kids in the box stand up and take notice of her a little bit.

Katie thought about all of this as she brushed her teeth, grabbed her backpack, kissed her parents and Neil goodbye, and jaunted off to school. She was still thinking about how it would be nice to be noticed a little for doing something of importance — like solving a mystery, when she found herself tapping on Mr. McKeever's open classroom door. Mr. McKeever was bent over his desk adjusting the knob of a microscope when Katie arrived.

"Good morning, Katie. What brings you to this bastion of knowledge so early?" he said standing up and turning to smile at her.

Katie found Mr. McKeever funnier than any other teacher in school, even though most of the other kids didn't. At least three times a week he would use a word or a phrase that the kids had never heard before (like bastion). It never failed that when he did, at least one student would ask "What's that mean?" When the question was asked, everyone knew what Mr. McKeever would say, "Expand your mind — fire your neural synapses!" Which every fifth grader knew to mean "Look it up in the dictionary!" Mr. McKeever was always kind enough to spell the unknown word on the board. Katie always copied the words down. She had left the back ten pages of her math notebook free to write down the words. She also never failed to look up the definitions; it just sometimes took her a few days to get to it. Most of the kids never bothered, and Katie couldn't understand why. She had heard from a sixth grade girl that Mr. McKeever gave an extra credit test at the very end of the year and the only things on it were the "expand your mind words." The girl had also said that Mr. McKeever never mentions the test until the day of it, and all students must take an oath not to speak of the test. Katie hadn't been quite sure why the girl had broken her oath and told Katie about it or whether the girl was just making it all up. Katie figured that she'd be ready for the extra credit test if there really was one, and if not, at least she had learned some interesting new words.

"Good morning, Mr. McKeever. I was wondering if I could come up during recess to do an internet search?" Katie asked a bit hesitantly. Katie knew that he might say no, but it was worth a shot.

"Well, you caught me on a good day. My wife is taking the cat to the vet at lunchtime, so I'm not going home for lunch today. I packed my lunch, and I'm going to eat here and grade some papers." Katie knew that Mr. McKeever usually walked home during his lunch period to eat lunch with his wife. That was the strange thing about living in a small town; you knew a lot about what other people did.

"Is your computer on the blink at home?" Mr. McKeever asked as he filled out a pass for Katie to give to the recess monitor. "If there's a problem, tell your parents that I can come take a look." That was a good thing about living in a small town— people did help each other out.

"No, Mr. McKeever. The computer is fine. It's just that we are going away tonight, and I won't have a chance to do a search on this thing that I've been working on," Katie was intentionally trying to be vague, and she was hoping that Mr. McKeever would just hand her the pass so that she could be on her way, but no such luck.

"Is this a project for Ms Carone that you're working on?"

"No. It's kind of a community interest thing. I'm really not sure if it's anything at all."

"Will it take you long to search?"

"I'm really not sure. I'm looking into something that happened a long time ago."

Katie was dismayed because Mr. McKeever took back the pass he had been about to hand her. Katie thought he had changed his mind about letting her use the computer, and she couldn't figure out why.

Mr. McKeever hadn't changed his mind, though; he had taken the pass back to write something else on it.

"Since your search might take you a while, show this to the lunch monitor and the recess monitor as soon as you get to the lunchroom. Ask to go to the front of the line. Tell them you are needed here as soon as possible. Eat quickly then come up and get to work," Mr. McKeever said kindly.

"Thank you. The extra time may really help."

"You're a girl on a mission. I can tell that. Let me know if I can help more."

"There is one more thing. How do you spell bastyun?"

Katie had difficulty paying attention during English and history, and that was unusual. Katie couldn't concentrate on what Ms Carone was discussing about last night's chapter of Frindle. When the teacher assigned them the next chapter to read over the weekend and had the students get out their history books, Katie didn't even notice.

Katie was still sitting with her thumb marking page 53 in the book when Ms Carone bent down and gently said in Katie's ear, "Earth to Ms Trout. Come in Katie. History book. Chapter 4."

Katie felt her face redden, but she could tell by Ms Carone's smile that she wasn't upset with Katie, just maybe a bit curious about what her most diligent student had been thinking about.

Katie quickly dug out her history book and caught up with the class as Ms Carone headed to the front of the room again. Katie glanced to the right and noticed Talia glaring at her.

Before Katie even knew what she was doing, her thoughts had turned to words.

"Look. I'm sorry you had to move. I'm not the reason for it. My dad isn't even the reason for it. Things just happen. You can hate me if that makes you feel better. But I'd like it much better if we could be friends."

It came out quickly and quietly, but with a lot of sincere emotion. Katie looked up and saw that Ms Carone was writing something on the board. It felt like time was standing still. Katie had said what she had wanted to say to Talia since Monday afternoon. She thought that her parents had been right in telling her to just ignore Talia, but there are only so many nasty looks a girl can take. Katie had said what she needed to say, and she had said it calmly and as kindly as she could. It was Talia's move now.

Katie hoped that the glare on Talia's face would loosen, but it didn't. If anything it grew nastier.

"It does," is all that managed to hiss through Talia's grimacing lips.

"'It does what?" Katie asked confused.

"It does . . . make me feel better--to hate you" Talia whispered leaning close to Katie and changing her grimace to a beaming smile. Anyone would have mistaken them for two best friends chatting in class.

"And. . . I'm going to go on hating you for as long as I live. The only thing that will make me feel better about what you and your family have done to me and my family is finding a way to make you pay. You think you're something special. You think everyone likes you. Well, that's going to change, and soon. Maybe even today."

Katie shouldn't have been surprised by Talia's venomous words, but she was. Katie somehow managed not to let a single emotion show on her face. She turned her focus to Ms Carone who was discussing something about how the House of Representatives worked. Katie was unbelievably proud of herself for not letting a single tear out. She would never give Talia the satisfaction of knowing how much her words had cut. Katie had learned in the last few days that Talia was mean, but she hadn't expected Talia to threaten her. Katie wasn't even sure what kind of a threat it was.

Katie thought about the rest of her day. She had this class, band, (and Talia wasn't in that class,) lunch, recess, and then Mr. McKeever's classes and gym. Katie took a calming breath when she reached her hand into her pocket. She had the pass from Mr. McKeever. Katie decided she would turn in her pass to the monitors and head directly to Mr. McKeever's room without lunch.

Talia's threat hadn't been a "meet me at the monkey bars so I can beat you up" kind of thing. Talia hadn't even been very specific about what was going to happen or where. For that reason, Katie didn't feel like she was being a "chicken" and not standing up for herself. Talia's words were just a dopey threat that she had come up with on the spot just to try to scare Katie. Katie decided it didn't really matter.

Katie already had someplace to be and something that needed doing, and she intended to do it, Talia or no Talia.

Chapter 17

Katie was in Mr. McKeever's room in record time after showing her pass to the monitors. There had been no sign of Talia anywhere. Mr. McKeever wasn't in his room when Katie bounded through the door, but to her surprise someone else was sitting down at one of the many computers that lined the tables along one yellow cinder block wall of the room.

"Why are you in here?" Hunter Thorne asked in a voice that sounded curious and irritated at the same time. Katie decided that he was probably just curious since his voice always naturally sounded irritated.

"I'm looking up some stuff on the internet. Mr. McKeever gave me permission. Why are you here?" Katie asked, curious, as well.

"Mr. McKeever has me practicing multiplication and division on this program that is kind of like a game since he says I don't know my math facts as well as I should. He told me to come up here and expand my stinking synapses during recess." Hunter said all this matter of factly, not embarrassed that he had to do some extra work.

"Mr. McKeever said that something is wrong with the power on that whole side of the room. If you're gonna use a computer, it has to be one of these" Hunter said indicating the three to his left and the two on his right. Katie noticed that the one on the left, directly beside Hunter was already turned on. Even though she wasn't enthralled with the idea of sitting right next to Hunter, she also knew that the computers at school took forever to boot up, so Katie opted to plop her books and herself down in that spot. Hunter had lost interest in their conversation and had resumed clicking on his math problems.

As Katie got to the search screen, Mr. McKeever came back into the room. "Heads up, knowledge lovers!" he yelled as he tossed a turkey sandwich and a small bag of chips to Hunter and then to Katie.

Katie's look of confusion made Mr. McKeever explain the food. "Hunter forgot his lunch money, so I told him to get to work, and I'd get his lunch—for which he must remember to pay me back. While I was down in the lunchroom purchasing said food, the monitor told me you had already headed up here, Katie. Since the lunch period had only started two minutes before that, I had a good feeling you had opted to skip lunch. That is a shameful way to treat your synapses! They need fed!" he said heading for his own paper bag.

"Thank you. I'll pay you back," Katie said graciously. She noticed that Hunter hadn't said a word up to that point, but after Katie spoke, Hunter said a sandwich-muffled "thanks," as well.

Mr. McKeever just nodded and motioned for both Hunter and Katie to get to work.

Katie decided to start with Olivia Dixon first. She typed in the actress's name and hit enter. Katie got hugely excited to see a page full of internet information with the name Olivia Dixon highlighted in site listing after site listing. Only when Katie looked closer at the first three did disappointment begin to seep in. Apparently Olivia Dixon was a relatively famous interior fashion designer from New York. Her comforter, sheet and towel sets could be purchased on-line or from large retail chain stores. When Katie clicked on the web listing for oliviadixonbio.com, it was not the Olivia Dixon she was searching for. The website told about the designer that was born in 1971 and who lived outside of Manhattan creating "the highest quality in living décor."

Every website Katie looked at only spoke of the designer Olivia Dixon, not the actress of the 1920's. That did tell Katie one thing. Her Olivia hadn't become famous like Virginia Kellogg, the other actress in the play.

Before Katie dove into a search for whatever local obituaries she could find on the name Dixon, she went to the wastebasket to throw away the plastic sandwich wrapper and the potato chip bag. When she did, she looked out Mr. McKeever's window and saw that her class was now at recess. Katie saw Talia standing by herself scowling and looking around. Katie had no way of knowing for certain, but she had a feeling Talia was looking for her. Katie breathed a sigh of relief for being right where she was, and headed back to the computer.

Katie entered the words "Ohio obituary Dixon" into the search rectangle and waited. There had to be close to a hundred listed, because Katie could tell that there were several pages to scroll through at the bottom of the page.

Katie checked first to see if there was an Olivia in the alphabetical listing, but there wasn't. Katie decided to take her time and go through the entries one by one anyway. At least Katie knew that she was looking for a woman alive in 1920. Olivia might not have been her real name. Heck, Dixon might not have been her real name either. Actors and actresses are known to change their names now; maybe they did that back in the 1920's, as well. It was even possible that since Olivia Dixon was an actress that traveled from show to show and from town to town, that she wasn't even from anywhere remotely close to Beech Grove, Ohio. If that was the case, Katie didn't feel as if there was much hope in the search, but she would give it a try anyway. Being a detective didn't mean that all the clues would just fall in your lap—like a program out of a grate. It meant that some serious searching that was sometimes tedious had to be done.

By the time that the bell rang to end recess, Katie hadn't had much luck. The only person she had found that had died anywhere near 1920 with the name of Dixon was a farmer by the name of Edmund who was only twenty-one. He had died of pneumonia in 1918.

"Head on out to your next class, studious ones," Katie heard Mr. McKeever say as she jotted down which obituary entry she had stopped on and closed out of her internet search.

"Mr. McKeever, you are our next class," Katie said with a smile. Hunter snorted a laugh. Katie wasn't quite sure at what.

"Right you are! I'm going to run to the office to make some copies. I'll be right back," Mr. McKeever said as he rushed out of the room.

"He's kinda squirrelly, but I like him," Hunter said unexpectedly to Katie.

"I do, too. It's a good thing, too, because he lives right down the street from me and his wife and my mom are pretty good friends," Katie said making polite conversation as students filed past them to get to their seats.

As Katie grabbed her books and headed from the computer table to her seat in the middle of the room, she noticed that Talia, who had already sat down at her seat two rows in front of Katie's, was smiling at her. It was the most wicked smile that Katie had ever seen. Something in Talia's face reminded her of a blurb that Katie had seen on the news last week. It had been about a fifty year old man winning the state lottery—about 17 million dollars. Katie remembered that on the news the man had been holding a big, oversized check and smiling a big smile. Katie had thought it odd at the time that the man looked like he was a mean guy for some reason, even though he was smiling. Talia had the same smile on her face--her eyes burned with hatred and her smile made Katie think that Talia had just hit the jackpot.

Katie found herself thinking—wanting to believe--that Talia really shouldn't be a threat, though. For the next two classes Talia was plenty far from Katie. Talia sat in the front row and Katie was two rows directly behind her. Katie breathed a sigh of relief. She had just about made it to the weekend.

Chapter 18

The last class of the day on Fridays for 5C was gym. Katie always thought of it as the most awful way to end the week. Most kids looked forward to Friday afternoons, because there was no studying, just games; Katie wasn't one of them since nine times out of ten, the game involved the word "ball." Today was of course, no exception: volleyball.

Since Katie had other things on her mind—the continued search for Olivia Dixon, the exhibit at the Bloomington Museum tonight—she decided that she wasn't going to let any ball get the best of her for forty measly minutes. Making things a little more of a relief was the fact that Mrs. Whetstone, the gym teacher, chose the teams randomly today instead of choosing team captains to do it. Katie, for once in her life was the third name called. On the down side, Hunter was on her team, and she wondered how many times she was going to get knocked down. There was one other good point—Talia was on the other team--all the way on the other side of the net.

Katie was the second one on her team to serve, and serving was about all anyone was doing. There wasn't much "volleying" going on. Even Hunter wasn't his usual obnoxious self. Maybe it was because the weather had turned lousy about half an hour after lunch. Storm clouds had moved in quickly and big drops of rain had been plopping on the windows in Mr. McKeever's room during math and science class. Now, in the gym, you couldn't see the storm that was approaching, but you could feel it everyone's attitude. It was either that or everyone was just tired of being at school.

The "ball" wizards in her class weren't much interested in the game, and quite honestly, neither was Mrs. Whetstone. At the halfway point, she let them all take a break and go to the water fountain to put off the remainder of the game for another few minutes.

Everyone lined up and waited for their turn to drink. She happened to be behind Hunter and that wasn't the nuisance it usually would be since today he was acting relatively normal. Katie felt a shove from behind, but didn't bother to look back. She just figured someone was getting restless since Jordan Bailey was taking an eternity to slurp from the fountain.

Katie felt the shove again, harder this time, and turned to see who it was. Katie knew she shouldn't have been surprised, but somehow, she was caught a little off guard. It was Talia--smiling that same wicked jackpot smile. She whispered to Katie, "Oh look, Mrs. Whetstone seems to have gone into her office." Katie could see Mrs. Whetstone through the glass window fidgeting with the manual pump trying to put air into the volleyball. Katie also noticed that she had shut the door. Katie didn't know what was coming, but she was certain something was, and it was unavoidable. She braced herself for another shove, or a punch or a kick.

Katie heard her dad's voice in her head and the words he had told her so many times. "You don't ever start a fight. Try to talk things out if there is a problem. You never throw the first punch, but if someone hits you, don't ever hesitate to hit them back. You have every right to defend and protect yourself." Katie felt her shoulders tighten. She knew that she couldn't turn around in line now, because Talia would do something, and probably make it look like an accident.

As Katie looked at Talia and thought about where to hit her once she was hit, and whether Talia's hit would be so hard that Katie might not have the strength to hit back, Talia did something unexpected. She spoke up so that the entire class could hear and she did so in a dangerously sweet, syrupy voice.

"I honestly could not believe it today, Katie, when I walked into Mr. McKeever's class and saw you holding hands with Hunter under the computer table. I had absolutely no idea you had a boyfriend. That is the sweetest thing!"

Immediately, the uninterested tone of the gym class changed. Murmuring and gasping started, and everyone began talking to each other all at once. It had the effect that Talia had intended.

Everyone was excitedly saying things like "Whoa, no way!" "Are you kidding?" "You must be joking!"

Talia spoke again, but directed her attention to everyone; her tone was sickeningly sweet, and laced with acid. "Oh, it's true. I saw it with my own eyes. They were holding hands and whispering to each other. It was enough to make you want to puke. I sit beside Katie in class and you should see the goo-goo eyes Hunter turns around and makes at her all the time."

Talia's words were greeted with another round of hushed, curious comments from the group.

Katie had no choice. She had to act. She wanted to punch Talia right in the face, but Katie didn't think that it counted that Talia had hit her first with words instead of fists. Katie looked from Talia to the group trying to decide what to do. She faced the water fountain and saw Hunter looking directly at her. The look on his face — one that she had never seen before — one of hurt and sadness-- made her want to cry. She felt the tears coming quickly and there was nothing she could do except move out of the fountain line and head to the restroom.

All Katie heard as she walked quickly down the hall away from her class was animated chatter.

In the restroom, Katie found herself crying, out of anger at the complete untruth of it all, but even more because of the look on Hunter's face. Katie knew that Talia's goal was to make Katie ashamed by associating her with Hunter. How the heck did that make Hunter feel? She knew because she saw it in his face. He felt like he wasn't worth liking. And Talia had made it so much worse. What every one of Hunter's classmates had been thinking for years, even Katie, Talia had put into words. That made Katie cry even more. That Hunter felt so awful about himself, and until today, Katie had been part of the problem.

It dawned on Katie that it was no wonder that Hunter acted the way he did. Kids, and even some of the teachers they had had in the past, treated him as if all he was a burden and nothing but a nuisance. It was not a surprise that he got in trouble a lot. If you feel that lousy about yourself, why would you put much effort into being nice to other people? Katie did notice that when they were in Mr. McKeever's room, Hunter acted perfectly fine, but then Mr. McKeever had a unique way of relating to students.

Katie decided to take a page out of Mr. McKeever's book and start being a little nicer to Hunter. No matter what Talia or any of the other kids thought. In her heart, Katie knew it was the right thing to do, and it took Talia's nastiness to make Katie see that she had, in her own way, been nasty, too.

Katie was a little astounded that she was able to work through all she was thinking in the girls' restroom. She decided that staying in there any longer wouldn't solve a thing, so Katie wiped her face with a cold paper towel and headed back for the last five minutes of gym class.

"Are you feeling better, Katie?" Mrs. Whetstone asked. "Some of the kids said you felt sick to your stomach."

"No. That wasn't it. I'm fine," Katie said in an unconcerned tone.

Katie vowed to herself that she would not let Talia or any other kid's teasing cause her to act in a way she didn't think was right. Katie was awfully glad that she realized this before she said something hurtful. It would have been very easy to say something like "Hunter is not my boyfriend. He's a complete jerk" when she was angry. Granted, Hunter could be a real pain and he was certainly NOT her boyfriend, a fact that was fine with Katie, but that didn't mean he should be treated like dirt. Katie was relieved that she had kept her mouth shut and walked away.

Tori leaned over to Katie when everyone was changing out of their gym shoes and whispered, "Katie, I know it's not true . . . what Talia said. Don't let her get to you. She's got it in for you, and I can't figure out why. You're one of the nicest kids at school." Tori stood up, winked at Katie and walked toward the steps to go to her locker.

Katie was surprised by the kindness and unexpectedness of Tori's words. Tori was a nice girl who Katie ate lunch with most days, but Katie had expected that when she left for the restroom and heard all of the chatter that everyone was laughing at her expense and Hunter's.

Tori must not have been. Hunter certainly wasn't. Maybe others weren't either.

Chapter 19

Katie felt shockingly lighthearted for having just half an hour before had a run-in with Talia. Walking home from school in the pouring rain would usually have made Katie grumpier than all get out, but fortunately, Mom had thrown a small umbrella in Katie's backpack just as she had dashed out the door this morning. Mom had said that she was certain that it was going to rain even though at the time there hadn't been a single cloud in the sky. Mom had also said that she wasn't going to let a single thing—not even a torrential downpour—interfere with their family evening out. Katie had rolled her eyes at her mother this morning for her goofiness—forcing an umbrella inside her backpack on a perfectly beautiful day, but she hadn't said a word. And now she was glad for the protection. Because of her mother, she wouldn't have to use the hair dryer when she got home, in addition to everything else she had to do.

Mom was already dressed in a blue floral blouse, black slacks and black heels when Katie walked in the back door, leaning out to shake the rain off the umbrella. Katie was pleased to see Mom wearing the necklace Katie had gotten her for Christmas and smiled as her mother's heels clicked all over the kitchen floor as she zipped around.

"I only need about half an hour to do my chores and get dressed," Katie said as she dropped her backpack and the umbrella by the door.

"I fed Diamond already and let him out. The rest of the chores can wait until tomorrow. You just get yourself ready. We can't wait too long—Dad's already in the van with Neil, and I see the wipers swishing about a hundred miles an hour. I'm thinking your dad is having second thoughts and may change his mind about going out to dinner, and I can't bear the thought of that! I'm heading out to calm him down. Get your behind out here lickety-split!" Mom said, smiling.

Katie kicked off her wet tennis shoes and ran upstairs to change into the silky lavender blouse that Mom and Dad had given her for her birthday and the black pants that she really liked. She had to dig in the closet to find the nice black shoes that had a little bit of a heel on them. She hadn't worn them in a few months, and Katie was relieved to find that they still fit. Before dashing back downstairs and out to jump in the van, she ran to Mom and Dad's room and gave herself a spritz of Mom's perfume, and then headed for the kitchen. She could hear Dad honking the horn for her to hurry up, and she took an extra second to rummage around in her backpack for her notebook and pen before she grabbed her umbrella and her jacket and locked the door behind her.

The hour drive to Bloomington was more enjoyable than Katie had anticipated. Typically Neil started to get wound up and fidgety about ten minutes into any car ride, and then, because she was seated right next to him, it automatically became her job to entertain him and get him interested in one of his many toys before he became an unbearable, raging toddler. This afternoon, Neil somehow miraculously managed to entertain himself with a book that he kept reading to himself. Katie knew he couldn't really read, but Mom, Dad and Katie had all read Hand Hand Fingers Thumb to him so many times that he had it memorized word for word. He even turned every page at the right time.

Katie didn't even mind listening to him read it for what had to be the thirtieth time as Dad maneuvered through traffic and puddles, because it gave Katie time to think.

When they got to the museum Katie knew it would be rude to run immediately to the exhibit she was so anxious to get a look at. She knew that she had to stick with her family. After all, it was a family night out. She hadn't yet told Mom and Dad about the exhibit that Mrs. Portage had mentioned, and she decided to wait until later. She was sure that her parents would give her plenty of time to look at whatever was in the exhibit when they knew why she was so interested.

Katie suddenly realized she had no idea where they were going to eat dinner. Since Mom was big into having a monumental evening out, it was possible that she had picked a restaurant to eat at that was far from the museum—it might even be in another town. That would give them less time at the museum.

"Hey," Katie said nonchalantly, "where did you guys pick to eat dinner?"

"There's a little restaurant called Mario's that your mom and I used to eat at every now and then when we were first married. I'm sure it's still there. There is no way it went out of business with as packed as it always seemed to be. You'll love it, Katie. They have every type of Italian food you can imagine, and burgers--all your favorites. The menu is huge."

Katie knew that Dad was trying to ease her mind because he thought that she was worried about it being a fancy restaurant that served caviar, liver goop, and all kind of other gross un-kid foods.

"Where is Mario's?"

"About two blocks from the museum. I'm hoping there is a parking space on the street somewhere in between the two; then we won't have to walk too awfully far in this weather. Was that lightning?"

Dad had indeed spotted lightning that unfortunately was right in the direction the Trouts were headed.

"This is bound to pass soon," Mom said hopefully. "For goodness sakes, it's been raining since 1:00."

Katie heard her dad quietly chuckling at Mom about how God didn't necessarily put a timer on the rain like they did on their lawn sprinkler, as Katie settled back for the rest of the drive, thankful that the restaurant and the museum were so close together, rain or no rain.

Dinner was absolutely delicious. Katie had pizza stromboli, salad and a piece of chocolate cheesecake. Mom and Dad really enjoyed their meals, too. Neither of them had been able to decide what to get when the waiter came to take their orders; finally, Dad picked fettuccini alfredo and Mom chose lasagna, and they agreed to split each meal in half and then trade. That seemed to have worked out well, because at dessert, they were still discussing the merits of each meal and having trouble deciding which one they had each liked best. Katie was having trouble figuring out how Mom was going to manage to get all the spaghetti sauce that seemed to be dripping everywhere down Neil off of him to make him presentable to enter the museum. Mom, however, had been way ahead of Katie, and was pulling out a small diaper bag and heading for the restroom with Neil in tow to change his clothes.

As Katie and Mr. Trout waited for Mom, Neil, and the waiter with Dad's credit card to return, Katie decided to talk to her dad about the mystery.

"Dad, if it's okay there is one exhibit at the museum that I am really interested in spending a little time looking at. . ." Katie's voice trailed off.

"'Infamous Crimes and Criminals—A Look into Ohio's Unsavory Notables,'" Dad said grinning from ear to ear.

Katie was startled. "How did you know?" she asked breathlessly.

"I ran into Mrs. Portage today at the produce stand. She said that she thought it sounded like we were in for a lovely night out, the four of us, and that she thought that there was one particular exhibit you might be interested in checking out, because it just might have a connection with your mystery."

Katie nodded, smiling.

"I told Mom about it, and that's why she was so keen on getting us moving so quickly after school. That's also why she thought to eat here tonight; so that you had enough time to do your investigating."

"Really? Thanks, Dad."

"Don't thank me, thank your mother. She's the one that came up with the plan. Hey, you need to know how proud both of us are of you. You are turning into quite the responsible young lady. Mrs. Portage couldn't say enough nice things about you this morning," Dad said looking genuinely elated. "It's really nice that you are spending time with her. She's a very kind lady, and it's a pity that her family doesn't live closer to her. I imagine that that is tough on her at times."

Dad paused for a moment before he continued. "You know, a lot of kids don't think much of older people. They think that somehow once gray hair and wrinkles appear, that intelligence disappears and that someone that's older doesn't have much worthwhile to share. But that simply isn't true. Older people may not be in touch with the music or fashion that is 'in,' but they have a lot of experience that we can all learn from.

"I remember growing up that I sometimes thought of it as a burden when my grandfather would sit me down and tell me stories about when he was young or offer me advice. Problem was that I never really bothered to listen to what he was saying. I was only interested in being polite and making the conversations end as quickly as possible so that I could get on with whatever it was that I wanted to be doing. Back then I was only concerned about what I wanted. Now I wish more than anything that I would have really listened to my grandfather then or that I had that time with him now, but none of us can change the past."

Dad looked right into Katie's eyes and beamed. "I am so glad that you learned that lesson early — to value people, to appreciate people — not for what's on the outside, but for what's on the inside. That is why your mother and I are so proud of you."

Katie felt her eyes welling up with tears. She hadn't thought it was a big deal to be friends with Mrs. Portage, and she still didn't , but it did feel good that Mom and Dad noticed things that she did and appreciated them.

Mom rushed up to the table with Neil trailing behind. He didn't look pleased to be unexpectedly shoved into his Sunday church clothes on a Friday evening. He might not know his days of the week, but he certainly knew that something was out of the ordinary since he was in what he called his "scratchy cwose" and the church was nowhere to be seen. Even so, Neil was in fairly good spirits — the pout on his lip didn't look like it would turn into a full-fledged tantrum.

The waiter returned with Dad's credit card, and Dad left the tip and signed the receipt in a flourish. Before Katie knew it, they were headed out the door of Mario's with umbrellas jerking in the wind as they scurried the two blocks to the museum.

Chapter 20

The storm seemed to only have gotten worse while the Trouts had enjoyed their meal. Lightning streaked in the sky above them and Katie had the feeling that the storm wouldn't be moving on any time soon. Dad held the big glass door of the museum open for Katie and her mom and Neil, who was attached to Mom's waist with his head buried in her shoulder.

When they entered the museum, Katie couldn't believe her eyes. Katie hadn't really thought about what to expect before they had arrived, but in the back of her mind she guessed that the Bloomington Museum would be something like the children's museum that was in the building next to the Deerfield Public Library. That museum had fluorescent lights in the two rooms that it filled. The fingerprint smudged glass cases there were filled with arrowheads and trilobites and bones that Katie had never believed for a second actually came from a dinosaur that was dug up around here.

The children's museum had been interesting to go to when Katie was about six, but its interest had only been worth one visit. Since it had been the only thing within about a hundred miles that called itself a museum before the Bloomington Museum had come into existence, Katie's mother had taken her several times to make sure that Katie got every ounce of education there was to be had there.

Katie supposed that she had expected some sort of bigger version of the children's museum when the Trouts walked in, and Katie couldn't have been more wrong. Just inside the big glass doors, there was a woman sitting in a small window-less booth. Her nametag said 'Julia' and she smiled warmly as she sold Katie's dad their tickets and then took their dripping jackets and umbrellas to hang on the racks that lined the walls behind her. Katie could tell before they even entered the big wooden inner doors to the museum that it wouldn't be very busy inside— mainly because it was a rainy, damp night and there were only about a half dozen other coats on the racks behind Julia. The storm must have made people opt to stay home and curl up with a movie or a book instead of venturing out into the world for some culture.

Katie was glad for the lack of crowd, she thought, as she stared up at the gigantic, glimmering chandelier that was above them in the entryway between the glass doors where they had come in and the large wooden doors they were about to enter. The rain outside and the dimly lit chandelier combined to make gentle moving shadow patterns on the dark paneled walls that Katie thought were lovely. She hadn't realized that Dad had moved ahead of them to open one of the big, wood doors, and that Mom and Neil had already gone inside. Katie rushed to catch up.

Katie hadn't had a clue what to expect inside. But what she saw was enormous. The museum was one giant room on the first floor with a huge decorative red-carpeted staircase in the center that led to the second level. The stairs were the only things that were carpeted. The light inside the museum was much brighter than in the entryway and Katie figured that that was a necessity since people were here to look at works of art and read about the exhibits. The wood floor was spotless and glistened in the light. There had to be thirty or more unsmudged glass cases in different areas of the room. Even though the room was open, there were large signs that indicated which areas held which exhibits.

Katie glanced at her watch and saw that it was only a little after 6:30 p.m. It had only taken them a bit more than an hour at the restaurant, and since the museum didn't close until 9:00, Katie knew she had plenty of time to see what she really wanted to see—the crime exhibit. Katie told herself not to rush. She was here to spend time with her family (even if the birds and whatever else was here weren't of much interest to her).

Dad handed Katie a program, and Katie gave a little laugh. The program was set up almost exactly like the one that she and Mrs. Portage had found at the historical society. Almost a hundred years later, and events still gave out information pretty much the same way. On the front of this one it said, "The Bloomington Museum presents our first annual Eclectic Autumn Exhibit." Katie laughed again because the word eclectic was unusual, and she actually knew what it meant—thanks to Mr.

McKeever and his synapse expanding words. Katie remembered the definition of eclectic that she had looked up: composed of material gathered from various sources. Katie guessed in this case that it meant that the museum had a bunch of exhibits gathered together that had absolutely nothing to do with each other.

When she opened the program and looked at the list of exhibits, she knew she was right.

> North American Birds — Fascinating Flights
>
> The Paintings of Aaron Stilman
>
> The History of Coffee: America's Beverage of Choice
>
> Entrepreneurs of Bloomington — Two Centuries of Sweat and Success
>
> Infamous Crimes and Criminals — A Look into Ohio's Unsavory Notables

After glancing at the titles, Katie got the gist of what the exhibits were about. Katie did have to ask her mom who Aaron Stilman was. Mom wasn't sure herself, so that was the exhibit they decided to check out first. It turned out that he was a local artist from the next county who painted mainly old barns and covered bridges. He had died last year, weirdly enough, in a barn fire on his farm and now his paintings were really expensive and something that everyone talked about. Katie found it really stupid that sometimes people were appreciated more after they were dead.

The only other exhibit title that made Katie wonder was "Entrepreneurs of Bloomington — Two Centuries of Sweat and Success." It took her a minute to remember, but finally the word 'entrepreneurs' clicked. Last year, she had learned it in a unit on economics in her history class. Entrepreneurs were people who started their own businesses. Of all five exhibits, that one sounded the absolute least interesting.

Katie didn't rush through the first exhibit. It surprised her that even though Aaron Stilman mainly painted only two things, barns and bridges, each painting seemed to have its own mood or personality; they really didn't look anything at all alike.

Next, the four Trouts headed to the bird exhibit. Even though it wasn't of huge interest to Katie or Dad, they did both enjoy watching Neil. In each glass case there was a beautiful bird sculpture that looked amazingly real, along with information about each bird. The cardinal and blue jay were Neil's favorites, probably because they were the most brightly colored. It was all Mom could do to keep his sticky little hands off of the glimmering glass.

In addition to the Stilman and bird exhibits, the coffee exhibit was the only other exhibit on the first floor. Katie was hoping her parents would be willing to pass it up or maybe see it on the way back downstairs, but she didn't hold out much hope since both Mom and Dad were avid coffee drinkers. As they headed toward the exhibit, Katie's mom noticed that Katie was beginning to get a bit anxious.

Mom smiled at Dad and winked and then said to Katie, "We're going to take a look at this exhibit. I have a feeling it won't interest you much, so why don't you head up to the criminal exhibit and we'll be up in a few minutes."

"You're sure you don't mind?" Katie asked with excitement.

"No. Go on. You'll probably be the only one up there, so it'll be quiet," Mom said as she tilted her head to the side at the five adults who had just come down the stairs and were headed toward Julia to pick up their coats.

Katie smiled and headed up the staircase. Behind her she heard Dad say, "Cappuccino, espresso ... What's the difference? Just give me a plain cup of joe any day."

Katie hadn't wanted to seem too eager to get upstairs, but she was elated that Mom had given her the opportunity. She was glad that she had thought to grab her pen and notebook before Dad had checked their coats.

As Katie reached the top of the staircase, she tripped on the carpet at the very top, not enough to fall, just enough to knock her pen and notebook out of her hand. The notebook landed at her feet, but the pen slid quickly on the shiny wood floor. It zipped about three yards to the right underneath a glass case. Katie grabbed her notebook and headed off after the pen that Mrs. Portage had given her. She bent down under the case and realized that the pen had slipped further back than her arm could reach. She decided to go around the back side of the case and kneel down to try to retrieve it from there. As she did, thunder like nothing Katie had ever heard shook the building. Katie wondered if it hadn't been thunder, but an earthquake, because Katie was certain that the floor was shaking and the glass case was vibrating. Katie grabbed her pen quickly and stood up, just as the lights went out.

"Are you all right, Katie?" Mom's voice echoed through the entire second floor.

"Yep. I'm fine."

"Stay right where you are. I don't want you coming down the stairs and falling in the dark. Just sit down somewhere. Dad is going to see if the ticket woman has a flashlight or if a generator will be kicking on."

Katie felt relief at the sound of her mom's voice, and did as she had been told. She sat down on the floor right where she was –not too near the staircase or the glass case that had been jiggling. Katie was just beginning to think that she should have asked her parents to see the criminal exhibit first instead of waiting through the Stilman and bird exhibits. If she had, she might have already found the information she was hoping for. Now she might not have the chance.

Katie heard footsteps coming up the stairs. There was a tiny beam of light, as well. Dad had two small flashlights with him.

"Here, honey," Dad said handing her one of the small lights. "The ticket woman said that we are more than welcome to stay even though there is no telling when the power will come back on. Mom and I are going to keep Neil downstairs because we're a little worried that he might fall down the steps if we come up here. We'll look around down there some more – probably at the birds he likes so much. You take as much time as you need up here to check things out. If you need some help, just holler down, but be careful not to bump into anything." Dad tousled Katie's hair and gave her a kiss on the forehead before he headed back down the steps.

Chapter 21

Katie didn't want to keep her parents waiting too terribly long—especially when Neil might be getting tired, bored and cranky, but she simply had to check to see if she could find anything in the exhibit about Olivia Dixon or William Tate – or pretty much anything with the year 1920 on it. At this point Katie would consider any little thing a possible clue.

Katie opened her notebook and made sure she had her pen as she pressed the button on the tiny flashlight and headed to look again at the glass case that her pen had slid under before.

The beam of the flashlight caused a great deal of glare on the glass, so it was hard for Katie to see very well. It got a bit easier as her eyes adjusted to the bit of light shining in the huge amount of darkness. The case contained a collage of old newspaper articles about a white man who had beaten up a black man in a parking lot in Deerfield in the 1950's. When the man went to jail, information came out about his involvement in the Ku Klux Klan and how he was trying to organize the group in the area. It had been a huge controversy and it had caused demonstrations in the community a long time ago. The backlash against the man had been so great that he and his family moved away after he had served his jail time. The title on the glass case was simply: "When Big Hate Hits Our Little Town."

The next part of the exhibit was a case filled with war memorabilia. The black and white pictures showed a lovely young nurse helping American soldiers that had been terribly injured in the war. Katie was a little confused as she looked at the items in the case--the woman's white nurse's cap, some old glass medicine bottles, the suffering faces in the pictures. Then she read the news article headline "Betty Silverman, Canton's Own Florence Nightingale, Convicted of Being a Spy." Katie noticed that the article was dated 1942.

To save time, Katie quickly went around to each of the cases and took note of what year each of the crimes took place. Even though she thought she would have liked to spend the time reading about each one, she knew she had to narrow down her search.

After passing other displays for a famous kidnapping in the late 1980's, and a company owner that had stolen millions of dollars from his factory workers' retirement accounts only five years ago, Katie found a case that she hoped contained a clue.

It was a display that was titled "Ohio Bank Robberies – Is Your Money Safe?" The display had no objects at all, just articles from different newspapers all over Ohio with different dates, one as far back as 1893, another as recent as 2006. There had to be at least twenty-five articles displayed in the case—most telling about robberies that had been unsuccessful. A couple did tell of robberies that had succeeded and how the criminal or criminals had managed to get away with the money. There were about seven of those articles, Katie guessed. Of those, most ended with no one getting hurt. There was one article that caught Katie's attention because of the year--not the year she was looking for--but it was pretty close: 1915.

Katie couldn't believe her eyes—even in the darkness with the tiny beam of light glaring through the glass, her gaze came to land on one word in the article—one name. "Tate" was spelled out in the same font as everything else in the article, but it seemed to Katie that the letters were bigger and bolder and somehow calling out to her.

Katie called her dad to come upstairs. She heard her voice calling him, but she couldn't take her eyes off the name. She felt like if she did, it might just disappear.

"What is it, Katie? Did you find something?"

"Yes, I think," Katie whispered, still not taking her eyes off the "Tate."

"What can I do to help you?" Dad asked excitedly.

111

"Could you read this article to me, and help me pick out the important facts? It's about a bank robbery that happened in 1915 in Rosewood, Ohio. Where is that?"

"It's about an hour north of Beech Grove. Hey, that's not a very long article and it looks like it's a copy already and not an original. The woman downstairs might let us make a copy of it."

"Do you think so?" Katie asked.

"Well, I don't think she's overwhelmed down there by the crowd. It wouldn't hurt to ask. I'll be right back."

As Katie waited for Dad to return, hopefully with the woman and the key to the case, Katie began to read the article, but the first thing she noticed when she was able to draw her eyes away from the name Tate, was that the person in the article with the last name Tate was not William. His first name was Jonathan. The robbery had taken place five years before the year she was searching for and the name of the person wasn't the same. Katie felt her heart sink. She thought she had found the piece of the puzzle that would make everything else just fall into place. It wasn't that simple, unfortunately. Katie did have a gnawing feeling inside that the clue wasn't a coincidence and that it did have something very big to do with her mystery. As Katie focused her little flashlight on the first words of the article, the tiny battery gave out and she found herself, once again, standing completely in the dark.

Katie stood still, patiently waiting for her father to come back. She hoped he would be able to convince Julia to make a copy of the article. That would certainly take far less time than standing in the dark with Dad's little flashlight flitting back and forth from the article to Katie's notebook so that he could read and she could write down the facts.

Katie breathed a sigh of relief when she heard Julia, the ticket seller/coat hanger, climbing the stairs. Katie smelled apple pie as Julia and her father got to the top of the stairs, and Katie realized that it was coming from the candle Julia was using to light her way.

"This is a very unusual request. Let me see which article you are talking about. If it is already a photocopy, I don't see any reason except for the fact that we are lacking electricity, that I couldn't make you a copy. If it is the original newspaper article, however, I'll need to talk to our antiquities expert to see if making a photocopy might compromise the artifact." Julia said all this as Katie's father led her to the display.

Katie smiled and pointed to the article, and Julia tried three different keys before the door of the case finally unlocked. Julia delicately took out the article that had been adhered to a firm backing so that it stood up in the case. She looked at it carefully and smiled back at Katie.

"I think it would be perfectly fine to make a copy of the article. I'll take it down to the office with me now, and as soon as the power comes back on, I'll have it ready for you. If the power doesn't come back on before 9:00, though, I'm afraid you'll have to wait to pick it up until tomorrow."

"Thank you so much for your help," Katie said grateful for Julia's generosity.

Julia headed down the steps with the article and her candle as Katie's dad thanked her, as well.

Katie suddenly realized that she hadn't had the opportunity to read the article yet. All she knew was that it was about a bank robbery in 1915 and that someone named Jonathan Tate was somehow involved. Katie decided against rushing after Julia to ask her to have another look at it.

Katie's dad must have been able to sense what Katie was thinking.

"Well, it's only about 7:30 p.m. We have almost an hour and a half until the museum closes. It's not a school night, so we could stay out a bit longer. Why don't we take a little drive around town and see if there is any place we could stop for dessert? Maybe the power will come back on in the meantime."

"We already had dessert at Mario's, Dad," Katie grinned.

"Finding a big clue to a hundred-year-old mystery deserves at the very least a small scoop of ice cream, don't you think?"

"You might be right, Dad," Katie said following her father's beam of light down the stairs.

The Trouts took their time driving through the dark streets of Bloomington looking for somewhere to spend a little time until the power came on or until it was 9:00 p.m. Mom and Dad pointed out places they hadn't been to in a while, or places where other buildings and businesses they knew used to be.

At 8:20 p.m., they found that they had pretty much covered every nook and cranny of Bloomington and the surrounding community, and there wasn't much left to do in the dark. The Trouts ended up right where they had started—in the very same parking space between Mario's and the museum. The rain had stopped, but the wind was still blowing strong. The soft music and conversation in the van had lulled Neil to sleep in his car seat.

Mario's seemed to be the only business on the street that had the forethought to have a generator. The lights from inside the restaurant were the only ones Katie could see except for the headlights of the occasional passing car.

Mom didn't want to wake Neil and have to deal with a tantrum—even if it was for ice cream, so Dad went in and ordered three ice cream sundaes to go. Mom said that this would certainly be a night to remember—a large power outage, sundaes out of Styrofoam hamburger boxes, and possibly the solution to a very old mystery.

Katie felt herself getting sleepy in the darkness of the van, listening to the wind and her parents' soft conversation, after she had finished her ice cream. Katie watched the numbers on the digital clock on the dashboard slowly flick toward 9:00 p.m.

She must have dozed off because the next time she looked it was 10:06 p.m. and her mom was gently rubbing her shoulder.

"Sorry, honey. The power in Bloomington was still out, and it looks like it is out here at home, too. I ran back into the museum to ask what time they open in the morning—10:00. I'd be happy to take you to pick up the article then, or if you want, you could go with Mrs. Portage. It's up to you."

Katie got out of the van, and managed to drag her tired, disappointed self into the house. She thanked her parents for taking her out, and made her way up to her room to change into her pajamas and go to sleep.

Chapter 22

Katie hadn't set her alarm clock the night before, but she was up and ready to face the day well before she would have been on a school day. Katie showered, got dressed, ate a yogurt, and was almost done with all of her chores before Mom, Dad and Neil even rolled out of bed.

Mom came into the kitchen to find Katie putting the last of the clean dishes away. "Well, you're certainly up and attum early," Mom smiled.

"I'm all caught up on chores. Can I go over to Mrs. Portage's now?"

"It's only 7:45, Katie. Don't you think it's a bit early?"

"I'm sure she won't mind. She said that I could stop by any time today. I know she's curious to find out what I found last night. I'll plan on going with her back to the museum this morning, if that's okay with you."

"It's fine. But when you get to Mrs. Portage's, if she isn't ready for company yet, come right back home. Understand? Here, take my cell phone with you. I'll be home hitting the housework all day today. Call if you need anything."

Katie agreed as she stuck the phone into her jacket pocket, slipped on her sneakers, grabbed her notebook and pen and headed out the door. At the end of the drive, Katie stopped, turned around and ran back into the house. Mom was pouring herself a cup of coffee when Katie dashed across the kitchen to give her mom a hug and a kiss on the cheek.

"Thanks for everything, Mom."

"Thanks for being a good kid, Katie. I hope the article has the lead you're looking for!"

Katie zipped back out the door and was on Mrs. Portage's doorstep before she even realized that she had run all the way there — and for once, she wasn't even out of breath.

Katie gently tapped on the door instead of ringing the doorbell, just in case Mrs. Portage had decided to sleep in.

"I'm coming, little one," Mrs. Portage hollered from the other side of the large wooden door.

Mrs. Portage unlocked the door from the inside and flung it open wide. "Well, this is good news."

"What is good news?" Katie asked.

"The fact that you are here this early. If you hadn't found anything last night, you wouldn't have been in such a rush at this hour to get your backside over here," Mrs. Portage chuckled.

Standing in the doorway, Katie told Mrs. Portage all about the name Tate, but not William, that she had found in an article about a bank robbery from 1915. Katie told Mrs. Portage that she hadn't had the opportunity to read it fully before the power outage, but that they could go pick it up this morning at 10:00.

"That is good news! I have a few errands I could run. Do you want to come with me? It'll help kill the next two hours until the museum opens. It'll be better than cleaning out flower beds!"

"That would be great, Mrs. Portage. You were going to check and see if you could find anything on the internet last night about Olivia Dixon and William Tate. Did you find anything?" Katie asked hopefully.

"Afraid not, little one. By the time I had the chance to sit down and do a search, that nasty storm had already started, and I had no internet connection at all, and then the power went out. Just when you knocked, I had tried again — nothing. The internet connection is bungled, but at least we have power this morning," Mrs. Portage said shaking her head.

Katie and Mrs. Portage spent the next two hours in a bigger variety of places than Katie would have expected. Not only did Mrs. Portage zip around on the road at a good pace, she had more errands than probably Katie's mom and dad put together. Katie had always thought that when people got older, they slowed down and spent a lot of time in rocking chairs. Well, maybe some people did, but certainly not Mrs. Portage. Together they went to the coffee shop to get Mrs. Portage a cup of coffee and Katie an orange juice, the post office to mail off a box to Mrs. Portage's great-grandchildren, and to the grocery store to pick up some odds and ends for a friend of Mrs. Portage's that had fallen last week and broken a hip. After they dropped those off, they stopped at the hardware store to pick up a small plastic ring to fix a leaky faucet in Mrs. Portage's bathroom. Then they headed to pick up some dry cleaning, and then to Mrs. Portage's church to pick up a plate that she had made a dessert on for a dinner the prior weekend. Mrs. Portage was considering stopping at the local gardening center to pick up some new gardening gloves when she realized that it was already 9:45, and although they had traveled quite a distance in the direction of Bloomington on the errands, they were still at least twenty minutes away.

Mrs. Portage was a little tired out after all of the errands, so she waited in the car right in front of the museum while Katie ran in to pick up the copy of the old newspaper article. Katie was delighted to see the giant chandelier in the museum entryway casting its warm glow—the power was back on in the museum, as well as everywhere else.

Julia smiled when she saw Katie come in. I just got here and made your copy not a minute ago. You sure are eager to get this. Is this for a school project, or something?"

"Something like that," Katie said. "Thank you so much for helping me. Can I pay you for the copies you made?"

"You're welcome, and no—anything to help out a student pursuing education."

Katie rushed back out to the car with the copy of the article. Since the original had been wider than a single piece of paper,

Julia had copied it onto two sheets. Katie had to overlap the pages to see the entire article at once.

Hopping into the car, Katie said, "Why don't we head back to your house, Mrs. P., and read the article there? That way, it's a surprise for both of us. If there is a clue in here, we can be excited to find it together, and if there isn't one, well, then. . . ."

"We can cry in our hot chocolate together, and then, wipe our tears, and hopefully connect to the internet," Mrs. Portage smiled. "You know, we can't be too disappointed even if there isn't a clue—we have only been on this case for less than a week! We must remember to be patient. Right, little one?"

"Right!" Katie agreed.

Chapter 23

"Have you ever heard the saying, 'a watched pot never boils,' Katie?" Mrs. Portage asked.

"Yep." Katie said as they both stared into the pan of hot chocolate Mrs. Portage was stirring on top of her stove. "I guess it really doesn't matter what's in the pot, does it? If you're waiting for it, it seems like it takes forever."

As Mrs. Portage got big mugs out from the cabinet above the sink, Katie went to her desk and brought the tape dispenser to the table. She placed the two pieces of the article together so that they overlapped just perfectly so that all the words could be seen, and then she taped them together—being careful not to read the article as she did it.

Mrs. Portage brought the steaming mugs to the table and plopped mini marshmallows in each cup while Katie got her notebook and pen ready to jot down important facts. Once both of them were finally seated, Katie passed the article to Mrs. Portage. Mrs. Portage cleared her throat and read the article out loud in an eager but hushed tone—almost as if she wanted to keep anyone else from hearing it, even though she and Katie were completely alone in the house.

Rosewood Examiner

June 9, 1915

The entire community is shocked and outraged by the violence and crime that came to our small town yesterday afternoon at 11:55 a.m. The Rosewood Savings and Loan for the first time in its 62 year history, was robbed. Had the crime been a mere robbery, our town could have recovered quickly, but we mourn today the tragic and unnecessary loss of life. Jonathan Tate, bank manager and respected member of the community, was killed during the robbery. Carleen Statford, a bank teller, gave this interview only this morning.

"A large man in a long coat came into the bank at about 11:45 with a leather bag. He stood at the table closest to the door for a few minutes with his back to us. He must have been waiting for the two other customers in the bank to leave. Mr. Tate had already let the other teller go to lunch since it wasn't very busy and he had said that I could go, too. He told me that as soon as the gentleman finished his business, he, Mr. Tate, would lock up and go home for lunch himself. I was just going out the door as the man approached the counter. I didn't really pay much attention to what he looked like. I do know that he was quite tall, had dark hair, a dark mustache, and a slight limp. About half a minute after I left, I realized I had forgotten my pocketbook, so I headed back into the bank. That's when I saw that the man had a gun and was pointing it at Mr. Tate. Mr. Tate seemed calm. He was handing the money to the man and the man was putting it in the leather bag. I screamed and then the gun went off. I ran to the police station as fast as I could to get help. When I returned with Officers James and Carlisle, the man and the money were both gone, and I was saddened beyond belief to see Mr. Tate's young son sitting on the curb right outside the bank. He had come as he did every day during the summer to walk home for lunch with his father. I'm not sure that he was there when I ran to find the police. I pray that he wasn't--I can't bear the thought of that boy having seen his father, such a good man, die."

Mr. Jonathan Tate, 37, is survived by his wife, Anna, and his three children. The suspect escaped with $8,000 in cash, the safety deposit box of Nathaniel and Mirium Pruitt, Rosewood's most prominent couple, and the security of our entire town. He is still at large. If any member of the community sees anyone matching the description Miss Statford gave, you are asked to get in touch with the police immediately. A reward is being given for the criminal's capture and the return of the Pruitt safety deposit box. Our thoughts are with the Tate family in their time of suffering.

"Oh, my word. . ." was all that Mrs. Portage could say for a long moment. Katie had heard the phrase in the past, but had never really understood what it meant. She still didn't, but she did realize it was what a person said when there was nothing else to say.

When Mrs. Portage and Katie were finally able to pull their eyes away from the article and look at each other, Katie saw the sadness in Mrs. Portage's eyes that she herself felt inside. It was amazing that something that happened to people you didn't know could make you feel sorrow almost a century after it happened.

"Oh, my word . . . can you imagine that poor child . . ." was all that Mrs. Portage could say quietly.

"If the boy was just sitting on the sidewalk outside, he must have been in shock. He must have seen the shooting or at least walked in afterwards and found his father," Katie said in an equally hushed tone.

Mrs. Portage pushed away from the table and went to the computer to see if she could get an internet connection. "Katie, what was the name of the bank manager? I know it was Tate, and it wasn't the William we are looking for."

"Jonathan," Katie said still thinking about the little boy. "This may just be a huge coincidence—the last names being the same, I mean."

"Yes, it may very well be, but the article really saddens me, nonetheless. I want to do a search to see if the culprit was ever brought to justice. I would just feel better if I knew what happened—that that little boy and his family . . . I don't know," Mrs. Portage said as she typed the name "Jonathan Tate" and "Rosewood Ohio" into the search box.

"You just want to know that things work out all right in the end," was all Katie could say.

The search turned up absolutely nothing. All that the search showed was a few articles from the last year and a half about a high school basketball player that was exceptionally talented in his sport at Rosewood High School. Katie figured it made sense; there was really no reason that the death of a man that was virtually unknown to everyone except the people of his small community would be entered into cyberspace ninety-some years later.

"I'm going to give Mr. Luckring at the historical society a call," Mrs. Portage said as she flipped through the pages of the phone book to find the phone number for the historical society once again. "Even though Rosewood is a bit of a distance from us, and not even in Lindeman County, he may have an old newspaper article about the robbery or he may be able to dig up some other information."

Katie listened intently to Mrs. Portage's side of the telephone conversation, and quickly her spirits began to lift. "Yes, Hello, Mr. Luckring. This is Mrs . . . Portage --- I actually told you my name was Pimplepuff before . . . well, that was because my friend Katie and I were working on a case . . . Why am I telling you my real name now? . . . Because I think you are becoming a critical part of our investigation . . . No, no, no, we're not investigating YOU . . . you're an asset is what I meant to say . . . we need your help . . . Oh, wonderful . . . yes, the information we found at the historical society was very useful, but we are in need of something else, and we aren't quite sure if you would have it or if you can help us . . . Oh, we certainly do appreciate that . . . yes, yes, well, we're looking for anything we can find about a robbery in June of 1915 at the Rosewood Savings and Loan. The bank manager, Jonathan Tate, was killed . . . Oh, I see . . . Really? . . . Yes, yes . . . I hope it isn't too much trouble . . . Yes . . . That soon? . . . Wonderful . . . We'll see you then . . . Thanks so much . . . Oh, well, I don't see why not . . . Yes, that would be lovely . . . Goodbye."

When Mrs. Portage got off the phone, she was grinning and giggling and blushing all at the same time. Katie didn't say a word; she just sat patiently and waited for Mrs. Portage to rewarm the hot chocolate in the microwave and come back to the table with their mugs and what Katie knew might just be some great news.

Chapter 24

Mrs. Portage was still smiling when she handed Katie her warmed up hot chocolate.

"That turned out to be a very interesting phone call, little one. I felt like I had to confess to Mr. Luckring about my real name— not the mystery. It didn't seem right to keep deceiving him. He is a nice man, a little gruff, but helpful. He said that he is quite certain that he doesn't have any information on Rosewood in his files, though I'm sure he can't be absolutely positive about that based on the state some of them are in, but he is more than willing to take a look. He did make a spectacular offer, though. He has a good friend that happens to be the curator for the Rosewood Historical Society, and the better news is that that historical society in the last month or so just finished scanning all of its old newspapers and other documents to make certain that they could be preserved for the future. Rosewood is a fairly large city and it has its own historical society, not merely a county one like ours.

"Mr. Luckring said that it should be no problem for his friend to do a quick computer search of their files and e-mail anything that might help us to him. The other good news is that both of the historical societies are open on Saturdays. I told him we'd stop by in an hour to see what his friend was able to find."

"Couldn't he have just forwarded you the e-mail that his friend sends to him?" Katie asked smiling. Katie was young, and even though she had only heard one side of the conversation, she was smart enough to know that Mr. Luckring liked Mrs. Portage and wanted to see her again.

"I'm sure he could have, but who wants to take the chance on important information getting lost out there in cyberspace? I think it is in the best interests of the investigation that we pick up the information personally," Mrs. Portage said blushing.

"What did Mr. Luckring ask you right at the end of the conversation?" Katie asked teasingly.

"I don't know what you mean," Mrs. Portage said — pretending to be confused.

"When you answered, 'Oh, well, I don't see why not . . . that would be lovely,'" Katie reminded her.

"Oh, that. He just wanted to know if he could take me out to lunch sometime to find out how it was that I got into the investigative business. I didn't think it was a bad idea. It's important to have contacts in our line of work, don't you think, Katie?"

"Oh, I do!" Katie agreed, glad that Mrs. Portage was making a new friend.

Since they had about an hour to kill until they went to see Mr. Luckring, Mrs. Portage made the two of them turkey sandwiches and broccoli cheese soup for lunch. Katie called her mother to let her know that they had already picked up the article from the museum, and it had provided some interesting facts that might or might not be related to the case and that she and Mrs. Portage would be heading out soon to go back to the historical society. Mom gave Katie permission to stay with Mrs. Portage until supper time, but only if it was convenient for Mrs. Portage. Mom didn't want Katie to "wear out her welcome," she said.

Katie didn't even bother to ask Mrs. Portage if she felt that Katie was hanging around too long, because she knew that Mrs. Portage was as excited by every chance at a new clue as Katie was.

After lunch, Katie did the internet search for Olivia Dixon and William Tate that Mrs. Portage had been trying to do last night before the storm hit. The search provided nothing at all of importance. The same names came up in articles here and there, but all of them were about other people. Katie knew this because there was nothing dated even remotely close to the 1920's.

The information that came from the Rosewood Historical Society was, however, a different story.

When Katie and Mrs. Portage walked into the same building they had just been in a few days before, Mr. Luckring was standing behind one of the tables piled with papers and what Katie thought was a computer and a printer, though she couldn't quite see them. In his hand was a single sheet of paper.

"I sure hope this helps. Phil, that's my friend in Rosewood, had no problem finding this on your Jonathan Tate. He said he read through this stuff and it gave him a few other ideas of things to search for you. He'll be e-mailing again in just a bit--if you have time to hang around," Mr. Luckring said gruffly, but with just a hint of a smile.

"We certainly do have time, don't we Katie?" Mrs. Portage asked. Katie just nodded, even though neither Mrs. Portage nor Mr. Luckring noticed.

"Is there a place that we could sit down and take a look at these, Mr. Luckring?" Katie asked not so much for her sake, but for Mrs. Portage's. Even though Mrs. Portage was one that could hold her own, (she had certainly proved that over and over again) Katie knew that she was feeling a little tired from all of the excitement and running around this morning, and Mrs. Portage probably was, too.

"Yep. I cleared off a place right over here for you. What was your name, kid?"

"Katie."

"Well, Katie, why don't you and Mrs. Portage call me Skip. If I am to be an associate in your future investigations, I believe we should be on a first name basis."

"That certainly seems logical," Mrs. Portage said. "You may call me Claudia."

"Is that your real name?" Skip asked, grinning.

Embarrassed for tricking him before, Mrs. Portage answered blushing, "Yes, it really is."

Mrs. Portage turned to Katie as they both sat down on two old bronze-colored folding chairs and said, "You know Katie, we are friends, and it never dawned on me to tell you that you can call me by my first name, but only if you'd like."

Katie thought about that for a long moment. She wasn't sure if it would feel right. Katie had always known the woman who lived down the street as "Mrs. Portage." But Mrs. Portage was right, they were friends, and maybe she should call her "Claudia."

"Honestly, Mrs. Portage, I don't know if it will feel right, but how about if I try it out a few times here and there and see."

"Now that's a good idea. Maybe if it doesn't fit for you, we could come up with a good nickname for me. I've never really had a nickname, well, except for what my oldest great-granddaughter used to call me before she could say "grandma" — Corky--how she came up with that I'll never know. It doesn't sound remotely like "grandma", but it sure is funny."

Chapter 25

Skip handed Mrs. Portage the paper he had been holding at the same time both Katie and Mrs. Portage opened their matching notebooks. It was becoming habit for both of them to keep the notebooks and pens with them and to get them out at the slightest chance of finding a clue.

What Phil had sent Skip probably meant nothing to either of the men, but it meant a great deal to Mrs. Portage and Katie. The page was exactly what Katie had hoped for: the obituary for Jonathan Tate. It was a bit blurry, probably because the newspaper that had been scanned had been so old and possibly wrinkled, but it was still completely legible.

Mr. Jonathan Tate, 37, bank manager for the Rosewood Savings and Loan, was shot to death Friday, June 8th by an unknown assailant. The shooting took place during a robbery at the bank. Mr. Tate was a well-respected member of the community, dearly loved by his friends and family. He is survived by his wife of nineteen years, Anna, and his three children, Benjamin, 16, Olivia, 15, and William, 13.

Both Katie and Mrs. Portage gasped at the same time. Skip turned around quickly from where he had been moving papers from one stack to another to see what was wrong. But what he saw made him shake his head in wonder: the woman and the girl were hugging each other and talking animatedly.

"I absolutely cannot believe it. . ."

"Both of them right there. . ."

"Oh, my word. . ."

"So they were both the children of Jonathan Tate," Katie said.

"Olivia's last name was different because she must have gotten married and changed her last name," Mrs. Portage said loudly and excitedly.

Just then, Skip came over with two other sheets of paper. "I just checked, and Phil did find a couple of other things. Here." He handed the pages to Mrs. Portage.

The first was the same exact article that Katie had found enlarged at the Bloomington Museum; the other page though was a follow-up article that was printed in the Rosewood Examiner on June 11th, 1915. Katie quickly surmised that in the few days that followed the robbery and shooting, something must have been discovered, because the article was longer than one that would merely have stated "Criminal Still at Large in Robbery Shooting."

A report was filed with the police on Saturday morning regarding the robbery of the Rosewood Savings and Loan and the shooting of Mr. Jonathan Tate. Theodore Trotter, proprietor of Trotter's Drug Store, told police the following: "A tall man wearing a long black coat came hurriedly around the corner of Main and Birch. I was on a small ladder cleaning the windows of the drug store when the man appeared from around the corner. He was not looking where he was going; instead he was looking over his shoulder. He ran right into the ladder and knocked me to the ground. I remember that he reached down, apologized and offered me a hand getting up. It must have jarred him pretty good, as well, because he was hobbling as he hurried off down the street. The other thing I remember is that when he spoke to say he was sorry, he had a very unusual voice. I'd almost swear that I'd heard it before. It was only a little while later that all the hullabaloo started around town about the bank being robbed. I didn't put two and two together until later when I read Miss Statford's description of the man. What she said jogged my memory – he was carrying a large leather bag. When he took off, he was headed in the direction of the train station. Of course that was the lunch hour, and the train heading south toward Baybridge would have been leaving just about then."

If you have any information about the robbery or the criminal, please contact the Rosewood police immediately.

Katie opened her mouth to speak, but Mrs. Portage stopped her. "Do you know where Baybridge is, Katie?"

"Yeah, that's not too far from here—only about half an hour away from Beech Grove. That's where my Uncle Tim and his family live."

"Right. Baybridge is north of Beech Grove. It's a little more than half way between Beech Grove and Rosewood. It used to be a fairly good sized city, but there was a tremendous fire at a huge lumber mill there around 1930. The houses and businesses were very close together and the fire spread like crazy. A lot of people were killed and those that weren't either didn't have their homes or had lost their jobs. The town pretty much disappeared off the face of the earth. Now it's just a few houses, a little grocery store and a big cemetery."

"That's exactly why Uncle Tim and Aunt Kathy love living there—because it is so tiny."

"I know this might be a stretch, Mrs. Portage, but is it possible that since Rosewood is about an hour north of Beech Grove, and Baybridge is about half an hour north of Beech Grove that the man that shot Jonathan Tate in Rosewood could have been headed down this way if he did take the train that afternoon?"

"Little one, anything is possible."

Chapter 26

"So let's just play a game called 'What If' right now," Mrs. Portage said. "The rules are that we just come up with things that could have happened, even if they are unlikely, based on what we know. And what is it we know?"

"That Jonathan Tate was killed in a bank robbery--most likely, though it hasn't yet been proven, by a tall man who had a limp. Jonathan had a wife and three children. L. might be short for Livy which might be short for Olivia and B. might be short for Billy and Billy is usually short for William. Two of Jonathan's children were Olivia and William. We have a note from B. to L. talking about picking up something important and getting out of town. The town, however, wasn't Rosewood or Baybridge or even Deerfield, it was little old Beech Grove. Olivia Dixon and William Tate were actors that traveled from town to town, that may have been brother and sister. They just may have been two of the actors in a play called <u>Now and Then</u> on Saturday, October 23rd, 1920."

Katie said all of this as she pulled the copy of the original note that B. had left for L. from the front of her notebook. Mrs. Portage was busy jotting down all the possibilities — not proven facts-- that Katie had mentioned.

"Did I miss anything?"

"I certainly don't think so," Mrs. Portage said scribbling.

"Hey, I did just notice something in the note that we overlooked before. Look here. *"If either of us doesn't make it, meet me at **home** where we found the big snapping turtle."* I didn't really think about that before, but finding a big snapping turtle sounds like something kids would get excited about. It sounds like that backs up our idea that they are brother and sister."

"You're right, Katie. So, let's start the 'what if's,'" Mrs. Portage said.

Katie was ready with pen in hand. These questions, like everything else, big or small, could lead somewhere important.

"What if the man that killed Jonathan Tate in the bank robbery in Rosewood hopped on the train and headed south to Baybridge?"

"What if William was the thirteen year old son of Jonathan that was sitting on the sidewalk in front of the bank after the shooting?"

"What if William saw the man and was so angry he wanted to kill him?"

"What if he somehow figured out who the man was?"

"What if the killer was an actor?"

"What if he later found out somehow where the man was and decided to make him pay?"

The barrage of questions stopped both Mrs. Portage and Katie dead in their tracks. They had been learning a lot of little facts bit by bit over the last week, now they were asking huge questions they weren't even sure were the right questions, much less if there was a way to find answers to the questions.

Neither Mrs. Portage nor Katie had noticed that Skip had moved nearer to both of them as they asked the "what if's." "I couldn't help overhearing, ladies, but that one question might have an easy answer, though I'm not quite sure. We could talk to Phil in Rosewood and see if there were any plays being performed around the time of your man Tate's death. It's just an idea."

"And a very fine one it is!" Mrs. Portage beamed. "Would you mind contacting Phil again?"

"It would be a pleasure, Claudia," Skip said as he headed off toward the computer.

As soon as Mr. Luckring had fired off an e-mail to Phil, the phone rang. Apparently, Phil, sensing something interesting was going on related to events in his town almost a century ago, wanted to be in on whatever it was.

As Mr. Luckring waited patiently for Phil to retrieve information from his computer with the phone tucked against his stubbly cheek, Mrs. Portage and Katie kept the game going.

"What if. . ." Mrs. Portage said thinking out loud, trying to spur another question.

"What if the guy that killed Tate didn't really mean to do it?"

"What do you mean, Katie?" Mrs. Portage asked as Katie dug out the copy of the first Rosewood Examiner article again.

"Remember, Miss Statford said, *'That's when I saw that the man had a gun and was pointing it at Mr. Tate. Mr. Tate seemed calm. He was handing the money to the man and the man was putting it in the leather bag. I screamed and then the gun went off.'* Maybe the guy just wanted the money and stuff and never wanted to hurt anyone. Miss Statford said that it looked like he was waiting for the other customers to leave and he came in at a time that some bank workers would be going to lunch. That doesn't sound like a man that is out to kill people. Maybe he just wanted—or needed—the money."

"You might be right."

"Oh, that might just help. Thanks, Phil. I'll print it out. Yep. I'll let you know how everything turns out or if there is anything else we need."

Mr. Luckring pressed print, and the printer spat out another, hopefully helpful piece of paper. Rosewood had apparently had a building similar to Beech Grove where all the big community happenings took place. But unlike Beech Grove and Deerfield, there had been a few theater buffs that had kept all of the memorabilia and documents related to plays and musicals carefully categorized and filed. In Rosewood there was an entire room with displays of props and costumes and a wall lined with posters from plays that had been performed. Phil had checked for plays being performed around June 8th, 1915 and had indeed come up with something.

On the paper was a brief write-up about a play called <u>The Quiet Room</u> that had been performed the two weekends leading up to June 8th. Mrs. Portage read the short write-up out loud.

<u>The Quiet Room</u> was far too dismal and silent for this critic's liking. The props were literally non-existent, and the plot of the play was barely present, as well. Daphne Bist, who played the leading role was far too quiet in her speaking, thus making the entire auditorium a truly quiet room. The only redeeming character in the play was the postman, portrayed by Thomas Madden, whose humor and charming stage presence, as well as his dramatic, booming voice, made this critic believe that it won't be long until we see this fine actor on one of the big stages of New York. In an upcoming critique, I will review the play <u>Onward and Upward</u> which is presently in rehearsal and scheduled for debut with a new theater troupe on our stage in two weeks.

Chapter 27

Katie was digging for the copy of the inside of the program from <u>Now and Then</u> and when she found it, she couldn't believe that what she hoped she would see, she actually did.

Thomas Madden

He had been one of the other actors in the play that Olivia and William had been in, but when she had done a search on him, nothing had come up. Now, here was his name again. This time, though, it was five years prior to the play in Beech Grove. He was in the same town, during the very same week that Jonathan Tate had been shot. If this was a coincidence, it was the biggest one in history, Katie thought.

Suddenly, Mrs. Portage was the one that had a revelation about a clue from earlier. "Katie, in the second article in the <u>Rosewood Examiner</u> where it spoke of the man knocking over the owner of the drugstore—the owner had said something about the man in the coat, something about his voice. What was it?"

Katie dug through the ever growing pile of paper clues and found the article, and found exactly what Mrs. Portage was talking about. Katie quoted the article. *"The other thing I remember is that when he spoke to say he was sorry, he had a very unusual voice. I'd almost swear that I'd heard it before."*

"Well, now, that seems to back up what the theater critic said. I know it's not a big deal, but it might be something," Mrs. Portage said shuffling through the stack to find the paper she had just read from moments before. "Here it is. . . *'Thomas Madden, whose humor and charming stage presence, as well as his **dramatic, booming voice** . . .'* It isn't often that a person's voice is mentioned as one of his or her main characteristics, but two different people commented about voice in this investigation, and it doesn't seem a huge stretch to think that both men might just be Madden."

Katie could only nod her head in amazement. She felt as if she were in one of the television shows her parents loved to watch where there's a crime, a few clues get found, and then in a great big swirl of activity during the last five minutes of the show, everything starts to fall into place, and as if by magic, the bad guy gets caught.

This, however, was no fictional story. It was something that had really happened to real people a long time ago, and the most amazing thing of all was that at least a tiny bit of this mystery had taken place in her very own home — the actor's boarding house.

Katie was wrapped up in her own thoughts, and didn't notice Skip and Mrs. Portage talking right next to her. She quickly tuned in to their conversation.

". . . that seems like a good idea. I think you might be right. When we found that program for your play a few days ago, we ended the search right then and there. There just might be something else if we do another search," Skip said.

Skip, Mrs. Portage and Katie took everything out of the 1920 drawer and divided it into three piles and placed each pile on a different part of the table that Skip had cleaned off. Silently each of them searched through their pile. Mrs. Portage and Katie did so quickly and eagerly, and then they traded piles to re-search each, thinking that they might notice something the other had missed. Meanwhile, Skip painstakingly examined each piece of paper carefully front to back, grunting and mumbling under his breath.

Katie and Mrs. Portage were almost through searching their stacks for the second time as Skip made a sound that wasn't his typical grunt or mumble. It was more of a gasp — the kind of sound Katie and Mrs. Portage emitted when they stumbled upon an important clue.

Skip's pile from the beginning had been more lopsided and sloppy than either Mrs. Portage's or Katie's, and as they stood looking at the bottom third of Skip's stack, they saw why. It wasn't a pile of regular papers. It was a pile of scripts — several from quite a few of the productions that had been performed in

Beech Grove. Quite possibly after a performance was over, some actors felt they had no need to keep the scripts since the entire thing had been committed to memory. Possibly some of the scripts just got lost in the shuffle of actors moving from one town to another. In any case, whatever the reason, there were about twenty scripts in a stack at the bottom of the pile.

Skip's gasp was because the very first one was a script for the play <u>Now and Then</u>. It happened to have the initials V.K. inside the front cover, and Katie remembered that Virginia Kellogg had been the other actress that had starred in the play, and she was the one that had become relatively famous, but had died in a car accident. Katie and Mrs. Portage looked over Skip's shoulder as he flipped through the pages of the script, but there was nothing terribly notable about it—only the lines that were Virginia's character, Cornelia Sankroft, were underlined. They looked at the back of the cover, as well, because, as Mrs. Portage and Katie had learned with the very first note that was found in the grate, important things could be written just about anywhere.

Skip gently placed the script off to the side in a pile all by itself, and then continued to look through the other scripts. Mrs. Portage and Katie stuck right with him.

In unison, they all gasped together, when about five scripts later, there was another <u>Now and Then</u> script. This one simply had Olivia written on the front cover. Again, page by page, the three of them went through the play. Olivia's had the same kind of underlining that Virginia's script had, but hers had a few notes in the margin, as well, and several little drawings here and there— like the doodles Katie saw her mom make on little scraps of paper when she was on the phone, and getting a little bored with the conversation, but not able to find a gentle way to end the phone call.

Mrs. Portage glanced through the rest of the scripts, but none of the others were from <u>Now and Then</u>. Looking at her watch, Mrs. Portage suddenly got a little flustered. "Good heavens, it is almost 4:00. Mr. Luckring—Skip—I am so sorry, I saw on the sign when we came in that you were only open until 3:00 on Saturdays—and look at us, we have kept you an entire extra hour."

Clearing his throat, Skip said, "That's no problem at all, Claudia. I'm just glad I could help. Let me know if there is anything else I can do."

"I certainly will and I'll let you know what we find out and where all this leads."

"I must admit, this little treasure hunt has gotten the historian in me very curious indeed."

"Well, I must be getting Katie home. Would it be all right if we took the copy of Olivia's script with us, if I brought it back first thing on Monday morning?" Mrs. Portage asked.

"I think that would be perfectly all right," Skip said smiling.

"Thank you, Mr. Luckring," Katie said very appreciatively.

"Skip. The name is Skip, kid. No more mister stuff, and you are welcome."

"Yes, sir. Come on, Claudia," Katie said to Mrs. Portage as they headed out the door and toward the car together. "Nope," Katie said honestly. "I don't know why it's not going to work, but I know for sure it won't. I'll be able to call Mr. Luckring Skip, but I just can't call you Claudia."

"That's all right, little one. Try out Corky next time. If that doesn't feel right, I guess we'll just have to find another one or stick with Mrs. P."

Chapter 28

Katie was glad she wasn't someone that got carsick when she read, because for the entire drive back to Beech Grove she read out loud to Mrs. Portage every single piece of clue they had--the very first note she had found in her grate, the Rosewood Examiner articles about the robbery and shooting, the obituary for Jonathan Tate, the review of the other play, <u>The Quiet Room</u>, that mentioned Thomas Madden, even their "what if" questions. Katie thought that if they kept going over everything, something more might just pop out that they hadn't noticed before. Nothing did though. Katie found herself thumbing through Olivia's script as they pulled up in front of her house.

"Corky, is it okay if I keep this for tonight and stop over and see you tomorrow?"

"Yes, you keep a hold of the script and take a good look at it for clues. I'm afraid I won't be home tomorrow until late. I am taking Evelyn to see her son tomorrow after church. She doesn't see so well anymore, and she is afraid to drive. Quite frankly, I'm glad to take her. She would be a danger to the community at large if she ventured out on her own. Her son lives quite a ways away, and I don't think I will be home until after dark. Why don't you see what you can find in the script and drop it off Monday morning before school, so that I can take it back to Skip?"

Katie tried to hide the little bit of disappointment she was feeling at not being able to see Mrs. Portage on Sunday as she got out of the car. As Katie shut the door and headed up the steps, Mrs. Portage pushed the button to roll down the window and yelled to Katie, "So..."

"So what?" Katie shot back.

"So how did it feel—calling me Corky?"

"Still not right. Maybe I'll try out a few of my own nicknames for you." Katie shook her head, smiling at her friend and waved goodbye.

Katie spent the evening playing with Neil and watching reruns of old sitcoms that Mom and Dad used to watch when they were younger. Katie loved her parents dearly, but sometimes she really thought they were squirrelly. They would go on these kicks where all they wanted to do was watch old Bette Davis movies or maybe it was a weekend to listen to only old country western music from the 1970's.

All the time she was with her family watching old <u>Brady Bunch</u> episodes and listening to her parents laugh, Katie's mind was somewhere else. She was starting to feel that this whole "mystery" thing might not be a mystery at all—just a way to conjure up adventure in her average, normal, eleven-year-old existence. She hoped that all of the curious coincidences that she and Mrs. Portage had discovered were not just lame attempts to make something exciting from nothing. Katie wasn't upset that the answers didn't just fall into their laps. After all, the whirlwind of the "mystery" had started less than a week ago; she just found herself hoping that there really was a mystery.

Katie thought to herself that she might just be thinking all these negative thoughts to protect herself—so that she didn't let her mind make this into anything too big, just in case, there wasn't really any mystery at all or just in case the what if's and what seemed suspicious all had perfectly reasonable explanations.

"Any clues today?" Mom asked, sitting cross-legged on the floor building a block tower with Neil. Dad looked from the television to Katie with a smile when Mom asked, eager to see what Katie would say—but trying not to look too eager. Katie was sure that her parents were very interested, but were pretending that this whole mystery was no big deal, so that she wouldn't think that they were trying to interfere.

Katie suddenly realized that even though she had been getting a little down about what might not be a mystery, her parents were still very interested in what was going on—and surprisingly in the last twenty-four hours since they had gotten home from the Bloomington Museum last night, quite a few possible clues had come to light that she hadn't had a chance to talk with her parents about.

Katie slowly began to recount to her parents what the article that they had found at the museum before the power went out said about the robbery in Rosewood. She told them about the obituary for Jonathan Tate and the article about the play The Quiet Room starring Thomas Madden—the other actor that was in the play Now and Then—that Mr. Luckring's friend, Phil had found. Katie also told them that she and Mrs. Portage weren't certain, but the L in the note might be short for Liv or Livy which was a nickname for Olivia, and B might be short for Bill or Billy which were nicknames for William, two of the other actors in Now and Then that they were pretty certain were brother and sister based on the reference in the first note to the snapping turtle and home.

As Katie told all of this to her parents, she found herself getting more and more excited once again. Katie realized by the look of disbelief on her parents' faces that all these small details seemed, when added together, to be more than just coincidence. She was once again certain of it.

"So let me get this straight. You think that the one guy that was in the play Now and Then here in Beech Grove—this Madden guy-- may actually have been the same guy that killed the bank manager at the Rosewood Savings and Loan in 1915? I know that the name Tate is probably pretty common, but the fact that one of the other people in the play that was performed here had the last name of Tate seems pretty incredible!" Mom said dropping the blocks in her hand and leaning back against the couch to consider all that she had just heard.

"Katie, if you don't mind me asking, did the Tate obituary mention the ages of the children?" Dad chimed in.

"I don't mind, Dad. Mrs. Portage and I can use all the help we can get." Katie dug through her notebook for the folded copy of the obituary—the same notebook that she had purposefully not been looking at for the last hour and a half. "It says here, Benjamin was 16, Olivia was 15, and William was 13."

"You know, back then, it wasn't uncommon for a young man to venture out on his own to make a living. If William had been thirteen in 1915, and let's just say for the sake of argument, that it was he that is the B. in the note, he would then have been eighteen in 1920 when the play took place here in Beech Grove. That seems a bit young now for a boy to be out on his own, but I don't think it would have been out of the question back then—especially if he was trying to find a way to make money for the family if his father was dead. Out of curiosity, I know you did searches on Olivia and William, but have you considered doing a search on Benjamin, the older brother mentioned in the obituary?"

"Dad, that never dawned on me. That's a great idea. Oh, and I didn't mention the script we found at the historical society today—amazing--it belonged to Olivia. That's funny—I hadn't thought of it until just now, but the script was probably here first, since this was the boarding house for the actors. Then it got moved to the historical society, and now, it's back here at our house again," Katie said as she pulled the script out from underneath her notebook. She didn't know why, but she had been avoiding looking at it all evening—possibly because she was afraid it was not really a clue—just a story in a faded paper cover that she was trying to turn into a clue.

Her parents' interest and her dad's suggestion to check into what happened to Benjamin Tate rekindled the fire and excitement that Katie had first felt when she stood on Mrs. Portage's doorstep and noticed the scrawled pencil words on the back of the piece of paper Monday morning.

"I know that you want to keep this quiet right now, Katie, and your dad and I appreciate you letting us in on it, but there is one other person you might want to talk to about this. Patty Thorne."

Chapter 29

"Mrs. Thorne? Mom, are you kidding me? Hunter's mom? Why would I want to talk to her about all of this?" Katie asked all three questions in rapid fire succession like a machine gun sputtering bullets.

"Pick your chin up off the floor," Mom said chuckling. "You might want to talk to her because of her family name. It's funny how sometimes you learn something that seems completely unimportant and irrelevant, and then shortly after, it comes up again. That was true about a word I heard about a week ago—obsequious—I had never heard it before and I liked the way it rolled around on my tongue when I read it in an article, and so I looked it up, and then the very next evening on Jeopardy that was an answer in one of the categories. . ."

Katie couldn't take Mom's rambling another second. "Mom, you're killing me. Why would I want to talk with Mrs. Thorne?"

"Oh, sorry. Because I ran into her when I was at the library last week. We got to talking about our families and where we were born, all that kind of thing. Turns out she grew up right here in Beech Grove and she gave me pretty much her entire family lineage, and one of the family names she mentioned—I can't remember whether it was a great-grandmother or a great-aunt, or what. . ."

"Mom, **please**," Katie begged.

"I am getting there, Katelyn. One of the family names she mentioned was . . . oh, somebody give me a drum roll, will you?" Neil heard his cue and began pounding blocks on the coffee table.

"Thank you, sweetheart," Mom cooed at Neil. "Twilly. Her family name was Twilly," she said smiling the same big dopey grin Neil was wearing. "I'm thinking if what you said was true—that the script was probably in this house at one time and had made its way to the historical society—Mrs. Thorne may know something about it. It was gnawing at me the last few nights since you first told us that this used to be Mrs. Twilly's boarding house that I had heard the name somewhere before, but I just couldn't remember where, until just a couple of minutes ago."

Katie didn't know if Mrs. Thorne could be of any help, and quite frankly, the idea of talking to the woman--the mother of Hunter--scared her slightly. She hoped that Mrs. Thorne wasn't as prone to shoving people as her son was. Katie thought that maybe it wouldn't be a bad idea if one of her parents went with her. Better yet, maybe Mrs. Thorne would just talk to her on the phone. Katie checked the clock above the television. It was already almost 9:00 p.m. She didn't want to call Mrs. Thorne before taking a little bit of time to think about what she would say first, and as interested as Katie might be in the answers Mrs. Thorne might possibly be able to provide, Katie wasn't quite up to tackling that project tonight.

Katie told her parents she would call Mrs. Thorne tomorrow and asked if it would be all right if she stayed up a bit and looked up what she could find on Benjamin Tate. Her parents agreed that she could work until 10:30 on the one condition that she would not give either of them an ounce of grief when it was time to get up for church in the morning.

Katie readily agreed and headed to the desk on the far side of the living room. It was nice that she had the chance to do a little research and still be in the same room with Mom and Dad. She was also grateful for the fact that it was 9:00—past time for Neil to be in bed. As she turned on the computer, Neil came over and hugged Katie, and said, "Lub you, Kadie!"

"I love you, too, Neil. Be a good boy for Mama and go to sleep, okay?"

"Kay, Kadie. Night."

Katie had to admit that even though Neil's main objectives in life seemed to be to drop toys all over the place and to torment Diamond, he was a good little kid. His cuteness made up for the fact that Katie was pulling chore duty for the both of them and probably would be for quite some time.

144

Katie realized suddenly that she had an hour and a half to work and three things to do—she wanted to make some notes for her impending conversation with Mrs. Thorne so that she didn't sound like a crazy person. She thought if she presented herself in an organized fashion, she might not tick off Mrs. Thorne. Katie also wanted to tackle the search on Benjamin Tate, and if there was time left, she wanted to look at Olivia's script again, to see if there might be anything important, since really, she, Mrs. P., and Skip had only taken a quick glance at it.

Katie decided that she could do the first two jobs at the same time. She typed "Benjamin Tate, Rosewood, Ohio" into the search box on the screen. She thought that there might be a good chance that Benjamin might have remained in the Rosewood area where his father had been the bank manager. Maybe if he hadn't lived in Rosewood, it was possible that when he died he might have been buried there. She might luck out and find another obituary.

Before she allowed herself to look at the web results, she jotted down notes to herself for her conversation with Mrs. Thorne. First, she thought she should explain that she was interested in the history of Beech Grove, and was considering doing a report for English class on fascinating places in town. No, even though it wasn't exactly a lie—she could do it for a future report—it would sound weird if Hunter heard, since the two of them had exactly the same classes. He might think she was some kind of freak that enjoyed doing extra homework. Katie decided against that approach. She opted to tell Mrs. Thorne what she had heard—that the Trout house used to be the Twilly boarding house. She would then simply ask if Mrs. Thorne could tell her any interesting stories about her home. Preparing for the upcoming conversation took only a few minutes, and Katie chose not to think about it any more. She didn't want to dwell any longer on the Mrs. Thorne she had allowed her mind to create: tall, grumpy, and pushy with a witch's cackle of a laugh.

Katie turned the page of her notebook so that she could write down any important details she might find on Benjamin. After about fifteen minutes of searching, and broadening her scope to "Benjamin Tate, Ohio," she found an article that was in the archives of the an old newspaper titled, "Oldest Ohioan to Graduate from High School is Seventy-Seven."

Benjamin J. Tate, known to his friends as Benny, is officially the oldest Ohioan on record to graduate from high school. Benny's friends and family were on hand to celebrate with him as he received his diploma from Wyethville High School. Benny said, "I am blessed to finally have this opportunity. When I was young, I had to get a job to support my family. It wasn't much of a job, just a farm hand, but the farm grew, and I was good at what I did. I always gave it my all. I became the manager of the farm and eventually owned that farm and the farm where I grew up. I started looking for new and easier ways to improve farm equipment and later I was able to start my own company. My only regret was that I never finished high school. Now I can say that I have. And let me tell you, if this old man can do it, anybody can!"

A graduation party and belated retirement party will be held for Benny on Sunday, May 29th from noon to 4:00 at First Baptist Church of Wyethville. All are welcome to attend. In lieu of gifts, Benny requests that money be donated to the Benny Tate Scholarship Fund at Crabtree Bank.

Katie quickly did the math in her head. If Benny was seventy-seven in this article that was dated 1976, then sixty-one years earlier, in 1915 he would have been sixteen. Even though the article did not mention any specific names of family members, it seemed very likely that this could be Jonathan Tate's oldest son.

Chapter 30

Katie decided that she would treat the article as a full-fledged clue, whether it really was or not. She reread the article for important details two more times after she had printed it off. In her notebook she jotted down what she thought might be of help:

*This Benjamin Tate would have been 16 in 1915.

*He had owned two farms and had started a business that had something to do with farm equipment.

Katie realized that the newspaper, simply named <u>The Chronicle</u>, that she had gotten the article from, if it was a bigger newspaper, could cover quite a large area — maybe even an entire county and then some. Katie also knew that the name First Baptist Church was very common — she attended the First Baptist Church in Beech Grove, and she knew there was another one in Bloomington. But Katie had a sneaking suspicion that the name Wyethville might prove important, since it followed the name of First Baptist Church and it was the name of the high school from which Benjamin graduated. Katie added "Wyethville" to the list of asterisks she had created. She also realized that she had never heard the name of the bank before. Since the article had appeared in the paper in 1976, it was very possible that the bank no longer existed, but doing a search on Wyethville and Crabtree Bank was definitely worth a shot.

Katie typed both words into the search box just to see what might come up. The first listing was for the Crabtree Banking Company of Wyethville, Ohio. When she clicked on it, up came the homepage for the bank where she could learn about how to open a checking account and what the current interest rates were. Katie didn't need any of that. She was just elated that the bank was still in existence. She wrote down the phone number and address of the bank, just in case she might need it. Even though she was only eleven, she realized that she probably wouldn't. If you called a bank asking about somebody that was or had been a customer, they wouldn't tell you anything — that was the law. Still, it wouldn't hurt to have it.

Next, Katie tapped in "Wyethville Ohio" and got what she hoped she would find. Since there was still a Crabtree Bank in Wyethville, it stood to reason that there was still a Wyethville. She clicked on the Wyethville Visitors Guide website. Katie thought that it was funny that a town that she had never heard of in her own state considered itself big and important enough to need a Visitors Guide. She could tell though, that it was a site that not many tourists probably took interest in since the calendar of local events was terribly outdated—almost two years. Katie's heart began to race when she found that the map on the website showed that Wyethville was the nearest town due east of Rosewood.

The site had listings for area businesses and things that might interest tourists—a bowling center, a park where the annual "Ladybug Festival and Rib Cook Off "was held, an outdoor flea market and farmers' market that took place every Saturday when the weather was good, and a farm where tours could be taken, pumpkins could be picked, a corn maze could be enjoyed, and children could learn first hand about how potatoes are grown and dug and turned into homemade potato chips. The name of the farm caught Katie's eye—"Taters"—it was probably a play on words since potatoes seemed to be a main point of interest on this farm that offered tours, and "taters" was a nickname for potatoes. But the fact that "Taters" farm had the name Tate in it and Benjamin Tate had been a farmer seemed too good to be true. Katie copied down the phone number and address of the farm.

Katie looked at clock over the television. It was 10:10 p.m. She had been working for over an hour and it felt like it had been about ten minutes. Katie decided to close down her search even though she still had a little time left. She spent her last twenty minutes talking with her parents about what she had found.

Katie's mom and dad listened intently, nodding their heads in unison—smiling eagerly, genuinely happy that Katie had had some luck in her search.

Katie realized that it was time for bed and that she hadn't had a chance to look at Olivia's script, but Katie was all right with that. The last hour and a half had been hugely productive—she thought she had the means to find out more about the man who might be

Olivia and William's older brother, and tomorrow she might have a better idea, after talking to Mrs. Thorne, about what used to go on in her very own house. Katie thought she would like to have a look at the script before church in the morning so that after church she could call Mrs. Thorne right away, so Katie made a point of setting her clock an hour earlier than usual, even though she was going to bed a whole lot later than normal.

The last thought Katie remembered having as her head hit the pillow was that Mrs. P., Claudia, Corky, Mrs. Pimplepuff (the names made Katie chuckle as she drifted off)—her friend, would be shocked by what Katie might have found when she heard.

Katie jumped out of bed as the alarm went off. There were some mornings when she woke up almost in a trance, not knowing what to do first—this wasn't one of those mornings. She had two full hours before they had to head out the door to church, and Katie wasn't going to lose a single minute it. No one was up yet, so she tiptoed down the hall to shower and get dressed. Katie usually showered at night, and her parents took turns in the morning. Katie hoped the sound of the shower running wouldn't wake them or Neil. After showering, dressing and brushing her teeth, Katie ran a brush through her chestnut colored, shoulder length hair. She had always wished for wavy or curly hair—hair like most of the girls she knew. But this morning, she was glad for her straight hair—all she had to do was put a little gel in it and brush it, and she wouldn't even need a blow dryer. It would be dry and look pretty good in time for church. Katie looked in the mirror and realized she had to work a little harder on being grateful for the things she had—like hair that she didn't need to spend a lot of time fixing—and try not to spend so much time wishing she had what others had.

Katie moved quickly and quietly downstairs—so far everyone was still asleep. She put on coffee for Mom and Dad, poured herself a bowl of cereal and sat down at the kitchen table with the script and her notebook.

Katie thumbed through each of the pages of the script — there were fifty-two and the print was pretty small. She looked at all the places Olivia had underlined what she had to memorize. Katie thought that it had to be pretty hard to pretend to be someone else, to try to feel emotions that weren't yours and to make them seem real to an audience. Katie couldn't quite decide whether that would be fun or not as she read the few small margin notes. The notes, in what had to be Olivia's handwriting, told her certain places to walk to on the stage, or certain movements to do as she spoke. Katie hadn't thought of that either — that not only did an actor have to speak all the lines that had been memorized, but the actor also had to move at the same time, making sure to do it the same way each time. If an actor did something different, it might throw off other actors in the scene and things could get pretty messed up.

Nothing in the handwriting stood out as being important to Katie, so she turned her attention to the doodles. They were little drawings made in pencil. On page three there was an old oak tree with a big hole in the center of the trunk and what looked like an owl peering out. On page thirteen was a small kidney-shaped pond with a farm house and barn in the background. On page twenty-nine was a drawing of what Katie thought was a book or a notebook with a leather cover and a buckle that closed it. In the corner of the cover were the initials O.T., and on page forty-four was a strange picture of a plain-looking box, and inside the back cover there was a larger drawing of a room, possibly the layout of the stage for the play. Olivia had been a pretty good artist.

Katie spent the rest of the time before church, as her family got ready, reading over every piece of evidence one more time. At church, she found that she really wasn't able to concentrate on the pastor's sermon. Her mind kept wandering back to the drawings in the script. To Katie they seemed very specific. When her mom doodled while she was on the phone, it was usually of different kinds of flowers with swirlies and curlicues around them. When Katie doodled in class on her grocery bag book covers, it was usually her own initials in big, chunky letters or geometric shapes of one sort or another. Olivia's drawings — the tree, the pond and farm house, the book with initials, and the box, seemed to have some hidden connection that Katie couldn't put her finger on — yet.

Chapter 31

After church, back at home, Katie changed into more comfortable clothes and took one more look at the drawings before getting up the courage to call Mrs. Thorne. She grabbed her notebook, pen and the phone book from the desk and headed to Mom and Dad's room, where she could make her phone call without any distractions.

After finding what she thought must be the Thorne phone number — it was the only one with the same first three numbers after the area code as hers--the numbers for Beech Grove, Katie took a deep breath and listened to five rings. It was 11:15 a.m., too late for most people to still be sleeping. Just as she was about to hang up, she heard a muffled "Yeah, hello. . ."

"Hi. This is Katie Trout. I am calling to speak with Mrs. Thorne." It suddenly dawned on Katie that she couldn't identify if the voice that had answered had been a man's, a woman's or a child's.

"Katie? Why are you calling me at home?" It was Hunter's voice. He didn't sound angry, just perplexed.

"Hi, Hunter. I'm not exactly calling <u>you</u> at home..."

"Yeah, ya are. This is my house and you just called it."

Katie began to get a bit flustered. "No, what I mean is. . . I wasn't trying to call you. I was trying to call your mom."

"Well, why didn't you say so?"

"I thought I did."

"Why?"

"Why what?" Katie asked, confused.

"Why do you want to talk to my mom? I didn't bug you at school or anything. There's nothing to tell on me about."

"No. I'm not calling to get you in trouble or anything like that. I found out that your mom's family used to own my house, so I wanted to find out more about it."

"What's to find out? A house is a house."

"Well, mine is pretty old." Katie tried to change the subject. "So how are your math facts coming along? Are you getting any better?"

"Yeah, I guess. I even practiced on the website at home yesterday — on a Saturday. Nobody at school would probably believe that."

"Sure they would. I do. Could I talk to your mom, now?"

"Yeah, hold on."

While Katie waited for Mrs. Thorne to come to the phone, Katie realized that she had just had an actual conversation with Hunter — the second one this week — and it had been relatively ordinary, normal even — a conversation like other humans have with one another. It gave Katie hope — not only was Hunter just like everyone else even if he had some horrendous social skills, maybe his mother was, too.

"Hello. This is Patty Thorne."

"Hi, Mrs. Thorne. I am Katie Trout. Andrea Trout's daughter, Hunter's classmate."

"Oh, yes. Hunter has mentioned you. What can I do for you, Katie?" Mrs. Thorne said warmly. Katie was doubly shocked, first at the fact that Mrs. Thorne had such a kind voice and second at the fact that Hunter had ever spoken her name. Why he would have done that, Katie had no clue.

"I know this might seem a little weird, but my mom mentioned that your family used to own our house — that it used

152

to be a boarding house. I kind of have an interest in history, I guess you could say. I was just curious if you had any stories or memories that you could tell me about my house." Katie tried to say all this nonchalantly, as if it were no big deal.

"Well, Katie. Your house belonged to my great-grandparents, Howard and Arlene Twilly. After my great-grandfather died, my grandfather changed the layout of the upstairs rooms so that my great-grandmother would have extra bedrooms and could take in visitors that came through town. That way, she could continue to make a little money to support herself. My mother used to say that she was a wonderful cook. She was able to charge more for her rooms than other places since her food was so great."

"Did she ever tell you stories about her house or the people she took in?" Katie asked.

"Well, she was very old when I was a little girl. I don't remember ever hearing her tell stories, but I do remember my grandfather—the one who worked on the house—telling stories. He lived a couple houses away from his mother and always tried to keep an eye on things. He was always making sure his mom was safe." Mrs. Thorne said all of this with a far away tone in her voice, as if she was remembering things she hadn't thought of in a very long time.

"He used to tell us how awful the house would smell sometimes—when his mom was canning sauerkraut or especially horseradish. The smell of the horseradish would hit you and make your eyes water before you even made it to the front porch. He used to say that her cooking had to be great to merit sleeping in a house that smelled like that at times."

Mrs. Thorne got quiet for a minute, and Katie had the sense not to interrupt; she just waited patiently, and in a moment, Mrs. Thorne continued, with a chuckle in her voice.

"I remember Grandpa telling us a story that seemed really peculiar and hilarious when we were young. Once there was an actor—most of the people that stayed at the boarding house were actors or traveling salesmen—that came to town. I have no idea what his name was, but Great-grandma said that he was tall, dark and handsome, very handsome. He was the kind of man that could sweep a girl off her feet. Great-grandma hadn't been one to often go to the theater, the opera house, to see shows. She thought all the acting stuff was a bit silly when there was real work to be done. Great-grandma was a real worker. Anyway, this good-looking actor got the best of Great-grandma. She couldn't resist going to see his play—in fact, she went two nights in a row. She would have gone a third, too, if it hadn't been the night that her applesauce needed canning.

"She was in the kitchen working away at just about the time the play would have been due to start when she thought she heard the front door open. That shouldn't have been the case since all four of the boarders staying with her were actors and they were all performing in the same play. Any other person coming to the door would have knocked. She went to check, but saw no one. A few minutes later, from the kitchen something caught her eye, and she darted out to the door. A tall woman was walking awkwardly down the street in the direction of the train stop. Great-grandma was mystified, because she was certain that the woman wasn't a woman at all, but the tall, handsome actor she had swooned over. The woman had the same slight limp as the man—especially when walking in heels, and he—or she—was carrying the man's burgundy suitcase. Great-grandma was confused by the fact that the person was heading toward the other side of town, away from the opera house. Great -grandma ran upstairs to check the actor's room, but all of his belongings were gone, and he had left payment for the room—and an extra $100 dollars on the bed. That was a lot back then. Great-grandma didn't tell the police right away, because the person really wasn't stealing. He was leaving with his own belongings and he had paid the bill. The only things he might have been guilty of were shirking his duties in the play and dressing very strangely."

The only words that kept echoing through Katie's mind were "handsome actor" and "slight limp." To Katie it sounded like Thomas Madden. Could it be that Olivia, William and Thomas stayed in the exact same boarding house when they put on the play? But if Thomas had killed their father, why—why would they be working with him and practically living with him?

Katie realized that she had tuned out on the stories that Mrs. Thorne was telling now — one right after the other. It seemed that Katie's question opened the flood gates to Mrs. Thorne's memories, and now there was no stopping her. Katie listened to several more stories — one about an Indian princess that had stayed at the boarding house for six months, another about a time when the old feed mill burnt down and all the houses, including Katie's, were overrun with rats. Katie patiently waited and tried to focus on the stories, but the one she was interested in had already been told. Katie found herself thinking about other details about the case when she realized that Mrs. Thorne had stopped telling stories and had moved on to something else.

"Yes, that was a huge family project. I was probably only about ten years old, but I remember that I thought I was going to die from all the hard work that week. Getting ready for an auction is no easy task, I can tell you. Sorting out things for family members, packing things up, cleaning the house. . . I remember thinking that Great-Grandma's house could have been a museum. I don't think she had ever thrown a thing away. There were so many strange little trinkets and things around the place that actors and salesmen would either give her for her hospitality or leave as payment or simply forget when they left." Mrs. Thorne's voice trailed off for a moment. "My mother had wanted to keep the house in the family after Great-grandma died, but all of the children had families and homes of their own. My mother had considered selling our house and moving into yours, but she decided against it because it was too big for her to keep clean, she thought."

Katie had been listening intently to this last part of the conversation, and finally chimed in with a question. "The little things that were left behind by the visitors, what happened to them?"

"I'm sure they were sold at the auction. There were a great number of scripts from the actors that were lined up on top of her piano in frames — my great-grandmother had a collection of those, why she had them, I'm not exactly sure, especially since she didn't find their profession to be all that impressive — except for the one actor I mentioned. You know, I'm not sure, but I think those were boxed up and given to the historical society since they were things that had to do with the community."

So that was how the script had gotten to the historical society after Mrs. Twilly's death.

Katie graciously thanked Mrs. Thorne for her time, and found herself thinking that the conversation, though a bit boring at times, was far nicer than she had anticipated, and it had certainly proven interesting—what with Thomas Madden dressing up like a woman and zipping through the streets of Beech Grove on a chilly October evening in 1920.

Chapter 32

When Katie told her parents all about the conversation—the unbelievably long conversation-with Mrs. Thorne, they couldn't help but laugh. After lunch, Katie couldn't help but think that as much as all of these little pieces seemed to be from the same puzzle, things were just not fitting together quite right.

The gnawing question seemed to be why would Olivia and William be acting and living in the same house with the man who most likely killed their father five years earlier?

Katie wished that Mrs. Portage was around today to talk to— just to bounce ideas here and there with.

Dad interrupted her thoughts. "Any homework this weekend?"

"Nope. Thank goodness."

"So you might have a little time to run with me to pick up a birthday gift for your mom?" Dad asked in a hushed tone.

Katie's stomach dropped. She had been so interested in the mystery, that she had forgotten Mom's birthday. Fortunately, she just needed a card—and to find a little frame. The present, the "Catorosities" copper nail plaque, was upstairs tucked away in her drawer.

Katie quietly told her dad what she had made and mentioned that she needed a frame for it. He told her to go up to the spare room where all the boxes were. There was a plastic storage box in front of the closet that had some knick knacks and frames. One of them might work, and if it didn't, they could pick one up on their birthday run.

Katie bounded up the steps and quietly opened the door to the spare room—the room she had only entered about twenty times in her life because her mother had fears of boxes falling and crushing Katie. It wasn't a "spare" room. Spare indicated space to her, and that was the one thing this room lacked. It was box after box piled up with roaster ovens and utensils and crock pots—all the things Mom needed for her business that she had no room for in the kitchen. She closed the door softly behind her so that Mom wouldn't come in and ask her what she was up to. She knew that Mom had come upstairs to treat herself to a nap after lunch and that she was right on the other side of the wall. Grown-ups were so strange in what they considered a "treat" to be. A real treat was ice cream or finding a new book by your favorite author or getting to stay up late. A nap was not a treat by any standard, except those of her parents.

Katie found an empty frame that would work perfectly in a matter of minutes. She stood up from where she had been kneeling by the box and looked around. This room would make a nice office for Mom and Dad if they could manage to clear it out. Maybe she would offer to help them with that. It would also need carpet or something. Katie realized, as she crossed the room to leave, why her parents had picked this room for the spare room and not one of the other three—the floor in here creaked like crazy. Katie felt as she left that she was in some kind of crazy obstacle course—trying to keep the floor boards quiet and the piled boxes from tumbling so that her mother wouldn't hear her.

Katie and her dad grabbed Neil and the diaper bag, left a note for Mom, and headed out the door to Supermart for birthday cards, a gift for Neil to give Mom and a cake. Katie thought for a minute that Dad might have forgotten until today about Mom's birthday, but he hadn't. He had specially ordered her a new mixer that she had been hinting around about since last Christmas.

At the store the three of them headed to the card section. After each of them had found a card, Dad and Katie split up. Dad took Neil to get Mom some earrings and Katie headed to the bakery to pick out a cake.

As Katie stood trying to choose between cake flavors and frosting designs, she felt as if she was being watched. Katie casually looked around, but saw no one that looked familiar to her. She finally decided on the chocolate-vanilla swirl cake with the white, pink and yellow frosting and she was asking the bakery woman if she could have "Happy Birthday, Mom" written on it when she felt someone directly behind her. As the woman behind the counter took the cake to decorate, Katie turned around quickly and found herself nose to nose with Talia.

Katie's first emotion was dread — she couldn't even escape the girl on the weekend — but Katie didn't let her face give away what she felt.

"What do you want, Talia?" Katie said wearily.

"Other than to make you miserable?" Talia hissed under her breath.

Talia had on her mean jackpot smile again. Katie thought that anyone watching must see how truly nasty she was just by the expression on her face. Because Katie was determined to stay calm and not stoop to Talia's level, she chose to force the most genuine, not over-the-top, smile on her face that she could.

"Here's the part I don't get. I already tried to talk to you about this. I am not responsible for what my parents do, just like you are not responsible for what your parents do. Why are you wasting your time being mean and looking for ways to get even with me for something I didn't do? Look, all the things you've done this week--the pencil breaking, the tripping at lunch, the making fun of my name, all of that is fine with me — if it somehow makes you feel like you are better than me, if it somehow makes you happy, great. But when you start involving other people — like the way you were making Hunter feel when you insinuated he was someone nasty to be associated with — that's rotten. I would take a Hunter that occasionally gets grumpy and shoves over a conniving, gossipy person any day. Maybe you should consider finding a new hobby, Talia. So far, you have been really lucky. I haven't mentioned a word to the teachers and no one has really seen any of the nasty tricks you've pulled, but sometime someone will, and that will get you into a whole heap of trouble.

159

Why don't you stop while you are ahead, leave me alone, and we can spend the rest of our lives ignoring each other?"

There had been times before in Katie's life when she had been angry, and when she was, she usually bottled the emotion up and later regretted not having said anything. This time the words came out eloquently, and even though she was angry inside the words didn't come out so. Katie's words sounded just like she felt—tired. Tired of Talia all the way around, and they had only known each other a week.

The woman behind the bakery counter handed Katie the cake and Katie thanked her and smiled. She had already turned away from Talia, and wasn't planning to look at her again. The bakery lady, she supposed, had heard the whole thing, and Katie thought that she saw the woman wink at her with a smile that said, "Atta, girl! Stand up for yourself and every other kid that has ever gotten bullied around!" Had she imagined the wink? The woman had already turned around at her table to decorate cupcakes.

Katie knew that Dad would be waiting in the frozen section trying to pick an ice cream flavor, so she turned to head that way. The punch was hard and hit her in the middle of her lower back. All Katie felt was the sharp pain and the cold tile as her cheek hit the floor. As she lay there, she felt the hot tears starting to come, and she tried hard to blink them away. It wasn't so much because of the pain in her back and on her face, as it was the fact that the cake for her mom, the woman that loved her so much, was in a heap next to her.

It was one of those times when even an eleven-year-old that's trying to be brave wants her mom or her dad—when she's just simply had enough. She looked around for her dad, but she had a feeling he was trying to avert a Neil tantrum that might be brewing if they were standing in an aisle surrounded by ice cream, popsicles, and every frozen treat imaginable. She was on her own to figure something out. At least she thought.

Chapter 33

"Could you, please, call the manager of the store and security to the bakery immediately?" It was a man's voice, but not her father's. But it was familiar and comforting. Someone was taking control of the situation, and for that Katie was grateful. Katie couldn't bring herself to look up; she didn't want Talia to have the satisfaction of seeing her cry. Katie got herself to a sitting position on the floor, and wiped her tears on her sleeve. There was blood on her arm, and she realized she must have bit her lip hard when she hit the floor.

"I don't know what you think you are playing at, but I saw exactly what you did. And let me tell you, if you think that I will let anyone lay a hand on Katie, you've got another think coming! Are your parents here with you?" the protective voice demanded.

Talia stammered quietly, "My dad is, but I don't know where."

"Could you, please, have a Mr. Blackwitt called to the bakery, as well?"

Katie heard the bakery woman call over the loudspeaker, "Mr. Slayman, Mr. Blackwitt and security to the bakery. Mr. Slayman, Mr. Blackwitt and security to the bakery."

"Sit down and don't move," the voice said harshly to Talia.

A gentle hand reached down and helped Katie to stand. The hand's owner had placed himself directly between Katie and Talia.

"Hey, kiddo. Look at me. It seems to me that you've gotten yourself into quite a conundrum."

Before she even opened her eyes to see who had come to her rescue, his choice of words told her who it was.

"I guess I have, Mr. McKeever."

The bakery lady handed her a paper towel for her lip and a sandwich bag with a couple of ice cubes to put on it when the bleeding had stopped.

Four men came from out of nowhere within less than a minute—the security guy with his hand on his holster (Katie almost laughed at how serious he looked and how terrified Talia looked), Mr. Slayman, the store manager, Mr. Blackwitt and Katie's dad, holding Neil. The look on Dad's face was one that Katie had never seen before—anger, terror, and concern all at once.

"I'm fine, Dad. Really."

"Really? Really?? You are bleeding from the face and you say, 'I'm fine Dad!'"

"Katie's got an owie!" Neil said, starting to tremble and on the verge of tears.

"Katie is okay," she said hugging Neil who was trying to kiss her lip, despite the blood.

Since Mr. Slayman wasn't exactly sure what the heck had happened, and because a crowd was beginning to gather, he asked all persons involved to go with him to his office. As Katie and Dad walked each holding one of Neil's hands, Mr. McKeever walked with Mr. Slayman and the security guard, talking seriously. Katie knew that Mr. Blackwitt and Talia were behind them, but she didn't much care. She was glad to have Neil's animated chatter as a distraction from her throbbing cheek, aching back and expanding lip.

When they got to the office, Mr. Slayman suddenly turned to all of them and spoke. "Mr. McKeever has told me what happened. He saw that young lady punch this young lady in the back. Katie, is it?"

Katie nodded.

"He had seen Katie speaking to the other girl—quite amicably, but seriously. When Katie turned and took the cake from Sharon, that is when the other girl punched her forcefully in the back. Is that what you saw, Mr. McKeever?"

"Yes, it is."

"Does that sound right, Sharon?"

Katie turned her head toward the woman she thought had winked at her before. "Yes, Mr. Slayman. If I might add, I did hear some of what this young lady, Katie, had been saying to the other girl."

"Go on."

"Well, I don't remember it word for word, but as I understand it this girl has been going out of her way to bother Katie for the last week or so, doing nasty things like tripping her at lunch. Katie was simply telling her to leave her alone."

"Is that right, Katie?" Mr. Slayman asked her.

"Yes."

"Is that how things happened?" he asked looking directly at Talia.

Talia shrugged her shoulders and sneered at the floor. Mr. Blackwitt, demanded in a low, muffled tone that she answer Mr. Slayman.

"Yes," Talia said in a whisper.

"Do you wish to fill out a report or press charges?" Mr. Slayman asked Katie's dad, as both Talia and her father whipped their heads up to see what his response would be.

Katie was certain that her gentle, kind-hearted dad would say that there was no need for any of that.

Looking directly into Mr. Blackwitt's eyes, Katie's dad said, "Yes, I do wish to fill out a report. I would like it on record what happened here today, so that if anything like this ever happens again, we will have this incident on file to take to the police. I am sorry, Mr. McKeever, but would you mind?"

"I would be glad to."

"If you don't mind, I would like to pick up another cake and take my daughter home."

"I am sure Mr. Blackwitt would be more than happy to pay for a replacement cake, wouldn't you, sir?" Mr. Slayman asked, or rather demanded in the form of a question.

"Yes. I am sorry, Dan. I don't know what has gotten into Talia lately, but I assure you, nothing like this will happen again," Simon Blackwitt said sincerely.

Katie's dad nodded his appreciation and thanked everyone, and as they walked away, Neil asked, "Kadie's okay now?"

"Katie's just fine," she said, feeling finer than she had felt since Monday afternoon.

"So I take a nap, like once a year, and when I wake up my child is bruised and bloodied. I swear I will never sleep again!" Mom said in an exasperated tone.

"She handled herself perfectly. You would have been proud of her, Andrea," Dad said hugging Katie's shoulder.

"Kadie's got an owie lip," Neil said excitedly.

"Obviously," Mom said sarcastically to no one in particular. "This all happened while you were out getting cake and cards for me? I am making a decree that we shall never again celebrate my birthday — in fact, I will never again have a birthday for as long as I live!" Mom said dramatically.

"Oh, Mom. Cut it out. Where are the candles?"

"In the second drawer. Now tell me the entire story start to finish, Katie, and don't you dare leave anything out!"

Normally, the Trouts would never have eaten cake and ice cream before supper, let alone instead of supper, but this was no ordinary day. After the celebration, and Mom and Dad checking Katie's back and head about a dozen times to make certain that she was only bruised and not concussed or fatally wounded, Katie headed to her bedroom, got out the gift she had made for her mother and put it in the old frame. It fit perfectly.

"Mom, I didn't have a chance to wrap this. . ."

"Oh, Katie, it is beautiful. Dan, take down that old gelatin mold from that nail on the wall. That will be the perfect spot for this. Oohh! Now we are an official business—we have an emblem, and everything! Thank you, sweetheart!"

"You didn't make that much of a fuss over the mixer," Dad said in a fake pout.

"You didn't make the mixer, dear. And Neil, give Mama a hug. I love the pretty earrings."

It was already 7:00 p.m. Katie had no homework, and Mrs. P. wasn't home, so Katie decided to head up to her room and, for what seemed like the zillionth time, look at everything she had collected in her notebook. Katie stretched out on her bed, lying on her stomach; her back felt a little less sore in that position. While she was looking at the Jonathan Tate obituary once more, she felt herself drifting off to sleep, but she didn't try to fight it.

An hour later Katie woke with a start and realized that neither she nor Mrs. Portage had ever bothered to read the script of Now and Then. They had both read the small synopsis about the play in the program that was written on the page with the cast list, but something about not reading something right in front of her made Katie uneasy.

Katie cracked open the script and spent the next hour and a half trying to picture two sisters that loved the same man and grew to hate one another. Katie was stunned that Olivia, playing one of the sisters would have had to have been snuggling up to Thomas in the play. She didn't know if it was possible to pretend to be in love with the man that you thought had killed your father. And William's role seemed equally strange. He played the long lost brother of Thomas' character who had been given up for adoption as a baby. His part required that he be overjoyed at finally finding his brother. This play and the people in it had "odd" written all over them.

Katie finished the play and realized that there was really nothing in the plot that could help her with her investigation. She decided to head to bed and deliver the script back to Mrs. Portage first thing in the morning so that she could get it back to Skip.

Katie showered, got ready for bed, kissed her parents and her brother good night and let her parents check her back, lip and cheek one final time for the night. Katie was becoming frustrated that the clues were so strange and tangled up, but at least she had the feeling she was on the right track. It just might take a while to get her train to the end of the line.

Chapter 34

At 3:00 a.m. Katie darted out of bed like a wild animal. Where was the script? Katie checked her desk, not there. She ran downstairs to check the kitchen table, her parents' desk and the coffee table, although she couldn't remember placing it on any of them. She headed back to her room and found it on her nightstand. Katie must have been reasoning things out about the mystery even in her sleep. Katie went through each scene of the three acts in the play to check the settings. What she thought she noticed was right. Every scene in the play took place outside in a park, or on a town street. Not that big of a deal, ordinarily, she figured. Plays scenes could be anywhere. What bothered Katie was that she was having trouble making sense of the back page of the script where Olivia had drawn the bigger picture of a room. Katie had thought that it must have been where the play took place, but now she knew that was not the case. So Olivia had drawn a picture of a room that had nothing to do with the play. But why?

Katie stared at the drawing. There was nothing particularly special about it. It wasn't like the kind of one-dimensional drawing of a blue print. It was not terribly intricate, but it was drawn from a unique perspective. It appeared that when you looked at it, you were in the doorway of the room. There was a closet to the left, a window on a wall across from the door and a window on the wall to the left. Down in one corner was a heating grate. The floor was made of wood and there was a light fixture that hung down in the center of the room. Katie suddenly felt nauseous. The light fixture was exactly like all of the lights in each of the bedrooms of her house; the heating grate on the wall in the picture looked strikingly like the one in her room.

Katie got up to stand in her doorway holding the script open to the back page with the drawing in her hands. The drawing looked strikingly similar to her room. In fact, it was quite amazing except for the fact that it was backwards — like a mirror image. Katie's heart lurched as she realized what she was possibly holding. She quietly tiptoed to the door of the spare room. She hesitated before opening the door, not able to believe that answers to her mystery might be closer than she had ever imagined.

The old wood door stuck tightly in the jam as it always did, probably another reason why Mom and Dad thought that it should be the spare room. Katie nudged it with her shoulder and flipped on the light switch. She stood in the doorway and looked around. This was the exact room in the small drawing. Katie found the same two words bouncing around in her head like tennis balls—but why? –but why? –but why?

Mom was pulling on her robe and yawning as she came out of her bedroom. "You okay? Do you need some pain reliever?"

Katie just shook her head and looked back again into the spare room.

"Cutes, are you sleepwalking? Can you hear me?"

"Mom, I'm fine. Look at this."

"Katie, I know it's a mess. We'll get around to organizing it sometime, but right now…"

"No, Mom. Look at the drawing."

Mom looked over Katie's shoulder at the script, and then looked around the room. "Oh, my word. Isn't that something?!" She whipped her head back into the bedroom and barked at Katie's dad—loud enough to startle him, but just quiet enough to keep from waking Neil. "Dan, get up. You've got to see this."

Dad didn't even bother with a robe. He was out of the room like a shot. "What? What is it?"

Mom pointed to the drawing, and it was an instant replay of Mom's words, "Oh, my word. Isn't that something?" And then he added, "That is too weird of a coincidence not to mean something. Kinda hard to go back to bed after that kind of discovery. I'm going to put on some coffee. Katie, I know that this is an odd suggestion, but do you think that you might want to call Mrs.

Portage? Even though it is the middle of the night, I think she would be excited to know that the drawing in the back of the script is an actual room in our house. Invite her over. If she'd like, I could go over and pick her up. Besides, you haven't seen her since yesterday, and I'll bet you have a lot to tell her about your discoveries. Make sure to tell her as soon as she answers that everything is absolutely fine. I'm not usually one who approves of middle of the night calls—they have a tendency to scare the wits out of people, but I think this merits an exception, don't you?"

Mom was nodding in agreement with Dad and Katie went to the phone in their bedroom and dialed.

"Mrs. Portage. It's Katie. Everything is all right. In fact, it's more than all right. I just discovered something and I found some other clues this weekend that I think will really interest you. Dad said you are more than welcome to come over right now if you'd like. He'll pick you up. And I had a little adventure today in Supermart that I want to tell you about. Are you sure? Okay. See you in a few."

Mrs. Portage had refused Dad's offer for a ride, and within three minutes she was at their door, fluffy slippers, face cream and all.

"We didn't scare you too terribly, did we, Mrs. Portage?" Katie's mom asked as she poured her a cup of coffee.

"Heavens no. This is exciting."

"Are you sure you weren't frightened?" Dad asked, chuckling. "It looks like we scared the color right off your face."

"Oh, very funny. This is my face cream. I wear it to bed every night to keep from getting wrinkles."

Katie was the one who chuckled this time. "Mrs. Portage, I don't mean to be the one to break it to you, but you already have wrinkles."

"I know, I guess I should have started doing this much sooner than three months ago. I'm just hoping it will fend off any new ones. Enough about my skin care treatments," she said wiping the cream off with a napkin. "What have you found?"

"First, Dad suggested that since we hadn't had much luck in our William and Olivia Tate search, I might want to check on the older brother. I did, and I found that a man named Benjamin Tate became a pretty well known farmer in Wyethville, the town right next to Rosewood. If it was the same Benjamin J. Tate — hey, the J. could stand for Jonathan, his father's name — he might have owned a huge farm that was called "Tater's." Get it, because it was a potato farm and his last name was Tate. I haven't had a chance to call and check it out. There was a phone number and address listed on the Wyethville website, but the website seemed a little outdated.

I also talked to Mrs. Thorne, a woman in town that Mom knows. Mom had found out, through the kind of bizarre conversations that Mom gets into with people, that Mrs. Thorne's family name was Twilly and that her great-grandmother was the Mrs. Twilly that owned this boarding house."

"Hold up, little one. I'm an old lady. Give my tired old brain a chance to get the caffeine pumping."

Katie was quiet for what seemed like an eternity while Mrs. Portage gulped coffee and looked off in the distance nodding with her eyebrows furrowed together, as if doing a terribly difficult math problem in her head. "Okay. I follow. Continue," she said seriously.

"Mrs. Thorne remembered her grandfather telling stories about the actors and other people that stayed in the boarding house. One was a tall handsome actor with a booming voice and a limp that one night BEFORE a performance dressed up as a woman and quickly left town. I am almost dead certain that it was Thomas Madden.

"I don't suppose that Mrs. Thorne knew anything specific like the name of the play the actor had been in or the year it was performed—just so that we could be certain we were dealing with the same person."

"No, the stories she was telling me were just passed down. Not really very specific."

"And look at this," Katie said moving closer to Mrs. Portage with the script.

This was the first time since Mrs. Portage had come into the kitchen that she had gotten a chance to look closely at Katie's face. "What the heck happened to you, Katie?"

"Oh, that's a story for later. Just let me say that the problems I had been having with Talia this week are probably over for good."

"That is good news. I just hope you didn't have to spend last night in the detention home to make that happen!"

"No, Mrs. P. This just happened today. I'll tell you all about it later. You have got to believe that this," Katie said shaking the script, "is far more interesting!"

Chapter 35

Mrs. Portage was now the one standing in the spare room doorway with the script in her hand, looking back and forth from the room to the picture. "Well, that is astounding!"

"Do you think this means anything?" she said pointing to a small squiggle mark drawn on the floorboard in the picture. It was drawn off center toward the left side of the room. It coincided with about the only clear walking space in the room. Katie went forward into the room to the general spot where the squiggle was in the drawing.

"Stop right about there. The drawing isn't exact, but you're standing on the squiggle spot, I'd guess," Mrs. Portage said. Each of Katie's parents was peering over one of Mrs. P.'s shoulders, nodding in agreement. From where Katie was standing, they looked like one person with three heads.

Katie looked all around her and from the floor to the ceiling. Nothing. She shrugged her shoulders, and took a step back toward the door of the room. Squeak. Katie gently rocked back and forth on the floor board; it made a noise that at any other time would be annoying, to say the least. To the four people now standing in the room, gathered around the spot, it sounded like music.

Mom ran to get a flashlight. Dad headed for something that could pry wood. Both were back in a matter of minutes--Mom with the flashlight from under the sink, and Dad with an arsenal of things that might be of use—three different screwdrivers, a crowbar, a hammer, a kitchen knife, and an electric drill. All four of them had given up the idea of trying to be quiet in all the excitement of possibility, and because of this, Neil had now joined the group. Mom grabbed the baby gate and secured it at the top of the steps. It wasn't all that necessary because Neil wanted to be near the action and the noise of tools.

"Katie, do the honors," Dad said handing her the crowbar. "Go at it. The worst it could be is a creaky floor board that needs replacing—but maybe it's something else."

Katie dug at the corner of the squeaky floor board with a flat head screwdriver. When she had made a space between it and the next floor board, she asked Dad to hand her the crowbar. She pried up and with one hard pull, the board cracked and broke off, leaving a hole in the floor like a small, dark box. Because Katie was on her knees in front of the hole and Mom, Dad and Mrs. Portage were all standing above her peering down, they blocked the light from the fixture above. Mom clicked the flashlight on and aimed it at the hole in the floor. Katie peered down and saw the edge of something that was mostly hidden back behind where the wood had broken off. That alone—just seeing a small bit of anything down there--was great. Finding nothing would have disappointed them all tremendously, after all of their expectations had been building up over the last half hour.

Katie reached her hand in and felt what was near the back of the hole. It was soft and pliable as she pulled it toward her. She had to bend it a bit to fit through the space she had created. When the object was finally on her lap, Katie recognized it immediately, though she could tell by their faces that Mom, Dad and Mrs. Portage didn't.

Mrs. Portage was still holding the script gently in her hands. "Mrs. P., take a look at page twenty-nine." Katie was surprised that she remembered the page number; she hadn't even tried to memorize it. Maybe she was more observant of small details than she had given herself credit for.

Mrs. Portage turned to the page and Katie heard all three of the adults around her gasp at the same time.

"That is simply amazing," Mom said.

Katie placed the leather-bound notebook on the kitchen table. All four of them stared at the initials O.T. in the bottom right corner that looked as if they had been burnt into the cover. The buckle that closed the book was well worn, as if it and the book had been used and well-loved by the owner for many years. Neil was occupying himself digging out every single toy in his toy box. He had a knack for doing this when no one was paying attention. And right now, all eyes were focused on the book.

Mom gathered in a heap all the papers, checkbook, pens and calculator from the left side of the table where she had been paying bills before bed — all without speaking or taking her eyes off the book. Dad poured coffee for everyone, and even made a cup for Katie with triple sugar and cream. Katie was pretty sure the counter had to be covered in coffee; since she was certain Dad had poured all the cups while still staring at the book, as well. Katie thought that all of them must be thinking the same thing: that if they took their eyes off the old leather-bound book, it might evaporate into thin air.

Katie knew they all expected her to make the first move. She sat down and each of them sat down, huddled close. It was hard to tell where one of their bodies left off and another one began since they were huddled so closely together. Neil had moved into the kitchen to annoy Diamond, who was sleeping peacefully in his dog bed.

Katie slowly unslipped the tail from the loop that held the book closed. She opened the cover of the book just as slowly. The pages inside were sewn into the binding. This wasn't the kind of notebook where you jotted something down and then ripped a page out. It was the kind that you wrote very important things in, the kind you expected to have forever. On top of the first sewn in page which Katie already noticed contained Olivia's handwriting, (Katie recognized it from the notes in the margins of her script), was a sealed envelope. On the front of the envelope were the words *"For You."*

Since the envelope was the first thing inside, Katie opened it first. Usually Katie was an envelope ripper, so much so that she often took off corners of her birthday cards in her excitement to get inside. This time, though, she knew better. Everything in front of her was old and worth preserving as much as possible.

Katie used the kitchen knife her dad silently handed her to wiggle into the corner of the envelope and slide along the edge. She pulled out the single yellowed page inside, and unfolded it.

Katie swallowed hard, and took a deep breath to calm herself down. She read what it said in a whisper.

I am not certain why I am doing this. You need to know before you read any further, that what you have found contains a story — my story. Please, I beg of you, keep it safe.

Katie felt the pieces that she and Mrs. Portage (and Mom and Dad) had been able to assemble formed the outer edge of a difficult puzzle. The pieces they had gathered were the easier straight-edged parts. Now, all of the inside of the puzzle might be about to slip out of a book and into the frame they had created.

Katie moved the letter to the side and turned to the first page. It simply said, *The Thoughts of Olivia Tate.*

Katie turned to the following page and saw that it, as well as quite a few that followed, contained simply labeled drawings. They were not as cleanly drawn as the ones she has seen in the script, and based upon what the pictures were of, Katie thought that these must have been drawings that Olivia had done as a young girl. The different drawings were jammed closely on the pages, turned sideways some places, drawn very tiny in others— as if Olivia's notebook was a prized possession that she had gotten when she was young, and she didn't want to waste a single bit of space in it. There were drawings of the same striped kitten over and over doing many different things—sleeping, playing with a ball, sniffing a flower, getting ready to pounce. Other sketches were of a farm house and a pond—it looked like it could be the same pond that was in the script because it had the same kind of kidney-bean shape. Still more pictures were of a boy with a dog, a vase of flowers, a birthday cake, a Christmas tree, a horse, and other various things.

"Olivia certainly loved to draw," Mom said as Katie flipped through about ten pages jammed full of sketches.

Chapter 36

Katie thumbed through the whole book for a quick glance. It was completely full except for the last five or six pages. After the first twenty or so pages of child-like drawings, the pictures lessened in number, but Olivia had begun writing down her thoughts. Katie thought that it seemed like a diary; most entries were fairly short. She read the first few out loud.

"Today it was really sunny out and Benny and me and Billy worked really hard to get our chores done fast because Mama said if we did, we could go to the pond and swim. Daddy brought home an old tire last week that he's gonna hang on a rope from the big oak so that we can swing out over the water."

"I hate rain!" was all another one said.

"David Danvers keeps pulling my hair and chasing me at recess. Benny says he likes me. I told Benny that if that's how he shows it, he's a big dope".

"Tabby, our mama cat, died today. I'm glad the kittens are a little bigger and weren't drinking her milk anymore. They should be okay. Billy said he would help me look after them."

Most of the entries were only one or two sentences in the first half of the notebook. They told of just ordinary happenings. Katie was tempted to skip ahead to the later pages where Olivia's handwriting looked more grown up, but she and Mrs. Portage agreed that it might be good to read everything from start to finish, just so they could get to know Olivia a little better.

At 4:40 a.m. Katie noticed that Neil had fallen asleep on the kitchen floor next to Diamond's dog bed. Mom told Katie that she desperately wanted to stay up and hear more, but she was meeting with a very high-strung, stressed-out bride to be in a few hours to make the final decisions about her wedding reception foods. Mom said she needed to get some sleep so that she didn't look like death warmed over. She gently picked up Neil, kissed Dad and Katie, and winked at Mrs. Portage.

She turned around again just as she was about to leave the kitchen and said to Katie, smiling, "Thanks for the most interesting birthday that I've had in my entire life!"

Katie kept reading and Dad and Mrs. Portage kept listening. As Olivia got older, her handwriting got better, and she included more details about her life. They learned that Olivia's mom was a great seamstress and made money for the family by making clothes for a Rosewood clothing shop. Olivia's dad was the bank manager of the Rosewood Savings and Loan, just as Katie had suspected. The Tates owned a small farm, but didn't grow a lot of crops; they mostly had cattle and pigs. Benny, Olivia's older brother, was a very hard worker that tried to take care of things after school around the farm so that his dad didn't have so much to do when he got home from work. Billy was the baby of the family and took full advantage of that fact. Olivia hated to sew, but loved to cook. And there were more and more entries mentioning a boy named Edmund that her father had hired to help out around the farm.

Without Olivia saying so in the journal, Katie could tell by how often Edmund was mentioned that Olivia really liked him. It was hard for Katie to tell how much time passed between entries in the journal. Olivia didn't write every day, that was certain, and she never wrote the dates on the entries like most people did in a journal. Olivia was growing up in a matter of hours in front of Katie, Dad and Mrs. Portage as they read her words, still, though, they could only guess how old she was.

The journal entries were now all at least five or six sentences, so the brief one Katie read next, hit them all like a box of bricks.

"Daddy was killed today at the bank."

Katie could tell by the spots on the page that Olivia had been crying when she wrote the words, and that the words hurt so much that she couldn't write any more. Katie looked up at her dad, grateful that he was just sitting there. The sad look on his face made the tears that were already pricking her eyes start to run down her cheeks.

Olivia said nothing more about her father. The entries that followed seemed to be about random things—a bake sale, the broken fence, Billy's ever-constant trouble at school, the fall mums blooming—anything that would help Olivia avoid writing about what was hurting her so deeply, Katie thought. The only semi-consistent topic that Olivia would mention was Edmund.

Katie gathered a little information about him through Olivia's comments. He was three years older than she was, and his family was the Tates' nearest neighbors. His family farm was about a mile away on the border of Rosewood and Wyethville. Edmund Dixon and his father didn't get along at all, so his dad thought it best if Edmund worked on other farms in the area, rather than the family farm. Mr. Dixon would pay farm hands to come work for him. Edmund thought that this was a ridiculous waste of money. Edmund couldn't make his father see that it was all right that they didn't agree on every single topic. Mr. Dixon was a very harsh man, and if you weren't with him, you were against him.

Katie got the feeling that Olivia knew that Edmund was rather glad he had taken the job at the Tate farm, because he was very fond of Olivia. Edmund helped Benny out more and more after Mr. Tate had died and they became very good friends. Olivia and Edmund would go on long walks after their work was done. Edmund built Olivia a cedar chest to keep all her special things in. Since many girls took cedar chests from home when they got married, Olivia wondered if Edmund was hinting around at something.

It didn't seem that Olivia had to wonder long. One entry said, *"I knew he would eventually work up the courage, and today was the day. Edmund and I will get married in the spring."*

Katie remembered that the obituary for Jonathan Tate said that Olivia was fifteen when he died, and that was in the summer. Katie still didn't know when Olivia's birthday was, but she was guessing that she must have been sixteen or seventeen when she got married.

"That is really young," Katie said.

"People got married much younger years ago," Mrs. Portage said matter-of-factly, not wanting Katie to stop reading, even though it was nearing six a.m.

"Dad, are you going with Mom to her wedding meeting?" Katie asked

"Nope. I'm here until she needs me to pack up for that volunteer reading program thing at 4:00. I was thinking, though, since you didn't get much sleep last night, what would you say if I said you could stay home from school today? You could finish reading the journal and take a nap later."

"Are you kidding me? That would be great. Will you call me off school?"

"Yep. I want to talk with Mr. McKeever anyway and thank him for yesterday. Besides, if you were sitting in class and managed to stay awake today, I don't think your mind would be on studying."

"Thanks, Dad!" Katie's eyes were burning from lack of sleep and squinting at Olivia's loopy scrawl, but it was definitely worth it. Having the day off school was an added bonus.

Chapter 37

Katie took a break from reading to get a shower, change her clothes and eat the pancakes Dad made for her, while Mrs. Portage walked home to get dressed and find her reading glasses. She refused Dad's offer of a ride home and didn't seem to care what anyone thought about her walking down the street in her robe and slippers. Mom woke up and padded downstairs eager to find out what was discovered in the short time she had been sleeping. Dad filled her in on the death of Mr. Tate and Edmund's proposal while Katie chewed.

Mrs. Portage was back and ready for action in about twenty minutes. Dad pushed a plate of pancakes in front of her, as well.

"Well, thank you Dan. I am a bit hungry, but I didn't want to waste time at home doing something as uninteresting as eating when I could be here!" Mrs. Portage must have been very hungry, because she and Katie finished their pancakes at the same time, and Katie had already gulped down half of hers before Mrs. Portage came in the door. Mom wiped off the table to make certain that there was no syrup to mar the old leather journal.

Mrs. Portage took over the journal reading for a while. A few entries were excited scribbles about the upcoming wedding. *"Mama finished my dress today, and it is perfect."* And *"Mama said that we can pick any piece of land we want to build our house on and Edmund isn't wasting any time—he's been walking around the property all day with Benny trying to decide where might be the best place."*

"Saturday, March 13th. This was the perfect day for a wedding. The sun was shining and I think all of Rosewood and Wyethville turned out to wish us well, even though only a few had been invited."

Still more entries like the ones before—ordinary, everyday things—problems with cattle feed, Benny's broken leg, the building of the house, how Olivia never appreciated all that her mother did until she had a house of her own to take care of, a wonderful banana bread recipe. In one entry, Olivia just raved about a play called <u>Cursed</u> that she and Edmund had gone to see in Rosewood. She thought the actors were amazing; Edmund thought the entire thing had been a waste of time and two dollars.

Olivia mentioned that she found it strange that Edmund and Benny had pretty much taken over each other's lives. When Mr. Tate died, Edmund was already working on the Tate farm and he continued doing more and more. When he married Olivia, he was family, so he took on still more. Edmund's father wanted nothing to do with him, and Olivia could never understand why. Mr. Dixon was an old man (Edmund had been the Dixons' youngest child) and he should have been relying on Edmund for help on the farm. Since Benny and Edmund had become best friends, and the Tate farm ran fairly smoothly under Edmund's care, Benny took a job for Mr. Dixon, one reason being it was so close to his own home, and Benny, more or less became Mr. Dixon's right-hand man. Benny always seemed confused by Mr. Dixon's anger toward his son—it really had no basis. Edmund was kind, a hard worker—a truly good man. Mr. Dixon's feelings baffled Olivia, Benny, and Edmund himself. The three of them could only guess that maybe Mr. Dixon had wanted a son that seemed tougher and not as tender-hearted, and one that kept his opinions to himself. Things continued on, though,—Edmund Dixon taking care of the Tate farm and, strange as it was, Benny Tate looking after the Dixon farm.

Still more entries. *"Edmund's slight cough has been steadily growing worse. He's been telling me it is nothing and he won't listen when I tell him to see the doctor. He has a fever and chills today. It is the first time he has ever stayed in bed. I called the doctor and he's stopping by."*

Another entry. *"It's pneumonia. The doctor says it doesn't look good."*

And finally, *"Edmund died."*

Sorrow seemed a constant in Olivia's life—first her father, then her young husband. Katie suddenly remembered something. She ran up to her room and grabbed her journal. She remembered seeing "pneumonia" and jotting the long word down but she didn't remember where she had seen it. Flipping through the pages of her journal, she spotted it, along with Edmund's name. It was the day she had been searching the internet in Mr. McKeever's room. Katie had merely written "Edmund Dixon 1918 died from pneumonia at 21." She hadn't jotted it down because it was a fact relevant to the case; she had noted it because it had been the stopping point in her search for the time being—a search she hadn't gotten back to, and now maybe, wouldn't need to.

Olivia mentioned in an early entry that Edmund was three years older than she was. Edmund died in 1918; Jonathan had died in 1915. Olivia was fifteen when her father died, so she would have been 18 in 1918 when her husband died.

The notes in the journal that followed were intermittent and Olivia's tone seemed terribly hopeless.

One entry stood alone on a page.

"Billy needs my help."

The next part of the journal seemed separated from the rest by not only a blank page, but also a lapse in time, just how much time, Katie couldn't be certain, but she had a feeling that what Mrs. Portage was about to read was exactly what the note that had been in the envelope had been referring to.

"Just start at the beginning…that's what my father used to always say when one of us got ourselves into some sort of trouble. Things seem to always make more sense if you tell them in order, so that's what I'm going to try to do. . ."

Olivia's tone had changed. In all the prior writings, it seemed like she was stating facts and telling things so that some day, maybe in her old age, she could go back and remember parts of her life. This last bit, just like the letter that was in the envelope, sounded different, as if Olivia were talking right to Katie.

"You need to know that at first, I was an unknowing participant. I almost wish it had stayed that way. The plan that we created may not

have happened as intended, but death was still the result. And I am a part of that.

I thought I had dealt with my father's death — as unfair as it was — and had put it behind me. The fact that the criminal hadn't been caught had angered me, but it hadn't consumed me — not like it did Billy. I worked hard to focus on other things after Daddy died, to start a grown-up life of my own. I thought I had that grown-up life with Edmund, but after he died, I felt lost and alone. We hadn't had any children. Children might have helped distract my thoughts. Children would have prevented me from being swayed by Billy.

Billy had always been a gentle boy. Always eager to please and willing to help with anything you asked him. He had been walking toward the bank the day Daddy was killed. He told me later that he remembered everything. He hadn't heard the gunshot, but he remembered Ms Stanford running out of the bank. He saw the man through the bank window. Billy hadn't noticed the mustache that Ms Stanford had mentioned when she reported the crime, but he had noticed the long coat, the dark hair, and the man's slight limp as he left the bank. He had watched the man leave through the side door, his arms heaped full. He saw his father slumped over the counter. He said that he hadn't been able to go into the bank. He didn't remember ever sitting on the curb.

After that day, Billy's demeanor began to change. He kept to himself more. If you asked him to help, he still would do so, but as soon as he finished he would usually go off on his own somewhere. I should have paid more attention to him. He was just a boy, a boy prone to thinking too much. Benny, being the big brother, could have taken on more of a fatherly role for Billy, I suppose, but he was so busy trying to keep the farm running. Mama didn't talk much at all; she just kept sewing. . .

I should have stepped in, but I was young and selfish. I focused on things that needed doing and more and more on Edmund. Billy continued to be withdrawn and gradually got into more and more trouble at school. Edmund tried to befriend him, but he seemed uninterested. He turned to books — reading anything and everything he could find — probably to escape his own life. Looking back now, I know that the books, the intricate plots and interesting characters, were encouragements to him. He had plans, too, but really no one to help him.

Then Edmund died. My grief tore at me day and night. I, like Billy, felt that I had no one. Mama had decided shortly before Edmund died that she was going to go live with her sister a few miles away. She couldn't continue to live in the house that she and Daddy had built together. Edmund's death didn't change her mind. I guess she didn't think that we needed her any more. Benny was old enough to take control of the farm, I was an adult – a widow that probably reminded her too much of herself, and Billy, he was too much burden and worry for her to bear. She half-heartedly offered to take Billy with her, but even Billy realized she didn't mean it.

I decided that since I should have looked after Billy better after Daddy's death, and now that Mama was leaving, I would make it right. Billy moved out of the house where we had grown up and moved in with me in the house that Edmund and I had built. Benny kept working – running both our farm and the Dixon farm, with some help from hired hands.

Billy and I would read stories and plays late into the night to distract ourselves from thoughts of the real world. I remember tidbits of conversations we would have about how fun it would be to travel, how interesting it would be to act.

Occasionally Billy and I would see concerts and plays that came to Rosewood – those evenings seemed to always rekindle the sparks of our prior conversations. Finally, out on the porch one evening, Billy said that he was seriously thinking of becoming an actor that worked in one of the traveling companies. He had no wife or children, as Benny now did, to tie him down. The meager amount of money he could make would well be worth the chance to travel and meet interesting people. He suggested I consider going with him. 'Liv,' he said, 'you are more beautiful than any actress we have seen on any stage around here. Any acting troupe would snatch the two of us up in a minute.' My reservations about his need to finish school were met with irritation. He saw no need.

I knew that the banterings of my little brother were not logical, and yet, part of me felt that it just might be what both of us needed – to get away from Rosewood, and the sorrow that lingered here. We told Benny of our plan. He was far from supportive, but he also knew that we were as bull-headed as he was, and that there wasn't much chance that he would change our minds."

Chapter 38

"Looking back, I should have realized that Billy was hatching a plan because some things fell into place for us far too easily. We spent two weeks traveling around the area seeing show after show to see which troupes had the most interesting scripts and most creative actors. Had we been in New York or Chicago, there would have been more options open to us. However, since we were plopped in the middle Ohio – we were limited in our choices. There were two groups. One group was comprised of six fairly well known amateur actors that mainly did comedies. They were looking for a man and a woman to join them. They were willing to pay $50 per week for each of us. The other group had lost three members recently due to a falling out. There was only a man and a woman left. They were looking for anyone willing to act, but were willing to pay only $35 per week. It was obvious to me that the first troupe was the better of the two. Without consulting me, Billy met with the other troupe and signed on. I didn't learn why for quite some time.

One night Billy asked me if I remembered Virginia and Thomas – the two actors we were now working with each and every day. When I told him I didn't understand his question, he told me that we had seen them on stage one night in Rosewood. Edmund had taken me to see <u>Cursed</u> and Billy had snuck into the performance after it had started and sat in the back. I remembered how much Edmund had hated the play and how much I had loved it. I hadn't realized that I was now working with two members of the troupe that I had admired.

Weeks passed and Billy seemed more animated than he had in a long time. He seemed eager to become friends with Thomas. Thomas seemed to want little to do with Billy. Virginia seemed to be only interested in herself and how pouty she could make her lips.

Another night Billy said to me out of the blue, "Thomas' leg seems to be bothering him more than usual. His limp is more noticeable. The man that killed our father had a limp." Billy's comment startled me, but Billy had gone back to memorizing his lines.

Billy and I both seemed naturals at acting. The memorizing of the lines came easier to him than to me, but finding the proper movements to match the emotion of words was my strength. After we had been with

Virginia and Thomas for almost a year, I realized that we knew about everything there was to know about Virginia – she thought that everyone she met was as interested in her life as she was-- but we knew very little about Thomas. Not for lack of questioning on Billy's part. We had learned that he had never been married. His mother had been sick and dependent on him when he was young. He had had a problem with gambling in the past, and he absolutely never read the newspaper. He couldn't handle reading bad news or bad reviews of his acting.

After one particularly probing attempt by Billy to learn more about Thomas, Thomas simply said, 'Kid, there are things in my past that I've done that I'm sure you might find fascinating, but they're things I regret. I'd like to leave them in the past.'

That would have been enough to squelch most people from digging further, but not Billy. He knew there was more to know, and he was on a mission to find it.

When we were performing in Baybridge, not far south of home, Thomas seemed particularly irritable the entire week. He and Billy fought over small, unimportant things constantly. It was strange. Thomas seemed on the verge of letting us know more about him, and even though that was what Billy had claimed he wanted, so that we could all work well together, Billy seemed agitated.

Finally, one night, Billy confessed to me that he thought Thomas was our father's killer. I remember that when he said it, I felt dizzy and nauseous at the same time. The declaration came from out of the blue and seemed completely unsubstantiated by fact. Billy went on to tell me about what he had seen the day that Daddy had died – things that he had never told anyone before. Thomas was the man. He was certain of it. Billy had recognized Thomas the weekend that Cursed had been performed in Rosewood – his limp, the dark hair. He would never forget the man that had killed our father, the man he had seen go out the side door of the bank. He had memorized Thomas' name, and found out from one of the other actors which towns the troupe generally performed in. That was the reason Billy had wanted to become a traveling actor. That was the reason he had wanted to join this particular troupe and not the one that paid a better salary. That was the reason that Billy was so merciless in prying out of Thomas every piece of information about his life. I should have known that Billy's interest in someone else when he was so self-centered had a motive behind it. He had, in his mind, *convicted Thomas of the crime, but was unwilling to go to the police. Instead, he was determined to carry out his own form of justice.*

I was angry at Billy for deceiving me — for letting me work with and become a friend to the man who might have killed my father. I was angrier still at Thomas for who he might be. I didn't want to believe it, but I found myself looking at Thomas as if he were already guilty.

Up until this point, I had been an unknowing participant in Billy's plan, almost an innocent bystander. Now I was becoming just as guilty as Billy of wanting to seek revenge."

Chapter 39

Mrs. Portage put down the journal for a moment and gave a huge sigh as she rubbed her eyes.

"I absolutely cannot imagine working with a person that you think killed someone you love. How could Olivia and Billy do that?" Katie asked, stunned.

"People do all sorts of strange things—especially when they are upset," Dad said. His voice sounded calm, but his face showed that Dad didn't really understand it any better than Katie did.

Everyone at the table offered to take over reading for a while, but Mrs. Portage said that she would love to continue for a bit, if no one objected.

"We finished the play <u>Now and Then</u> in Baybridge and moved on to Beech Grove to perform it once more. The stage in Beech Grove was larger, so it gave the opportunity to expand two of the scenes and create a bigger set. That was the responsibility of the community actors and the director. Since the four of us had already memorized our parts and performed it several times before, we had more free time than we had had in several weeks.

Billy knew that Thomas was a theater buff through and through, and even though it was not necessary that he be at the theater while the sets were being completed, he couldn't resist. The night we were to perform, after our final afternoon practice, Billy crept into Thomas' room when he was certain Thomas would be at the theater and searched. He wanted some evidence that he, indeed, did have the right man. He found what he was looking for. A metal box pushed back to the far corner under the bed. Even though the box didn't have the name on it, Billy was certain it was the Pruitt safety deposit box that had been taken during the robbery. The original lock had been broken, probably since Thomas hadn't had time to demand the key in his haste. The box was held closed with a new flipping clasp device that Thomas must have put on himself. Billy told me he didn't think twice about looking in someone else's belongings—mainly because he was certain what he was looking at didn't belong to Thomas either.

Inside was a huge amount of money – probably the last thing our father had ever touched – a gun, a diamond necklace, two folded stocks for a company Billy had never heard of, and an envelope. For Billy, it was enough evidence. He closed the box, flipped the clasp, and put the box back where he had found it.

Billy came and told me what he had found. We made a plan to perform the play as usual and during the night, kill Thomas and take the box. If we smothered him with a pillow we thought it might look like he had died naturally. We could stay in Beech Grove a few days acting shocked and sorrowful.

Looking back, I think that Thomas must have suspected something. Billy and I thought we were so clever, but if we had truly been clever, we would have thought to have Billy take a stage name, rather than keep Tate, the last name of the man that Thomas Madden had killed. Granted Tate is a common name. The fact that Thomas was not prone to reading newspapers, and probably had never even known the name of the man he killed or the family he had destroyed, was to our advantage. The fact that we were prying into the life of a man that had committed a murder and had been hiding out – almost in plain sight for five years – a man that might have a keen sense of self-preservation was working against us.

All I know is that Billy suspected that Thomas knew something was not quite as it should be. Maybe I was quieter than usual; maybe Billy was too talkative; maybe Billy and I glanced at each other too many times at dinner; maybe Thomas saw the note before I did. I will never know exactly what made Thomas nervous, but something did.

After Mrs. Twilly had served an early dinner to us, I went out for a short walk to clear my head. Planning a murder and preparing for a play was more than I could handle. By the time I returned, I had thought things through and had come to my senses. Thinking about killing someone, planning to kill someone, was as far as I could go. My rage toward Thomas hadn't subsided, but the police could take care of him. I knew I wasn't a killer. I knew I couldn't do it, or be any part of it, and I had to tell Billy.

I had only about fifteen minutes until I had to be at the Opera House to get into my make up and costume. Billy was not in his room. I knew I would still have time to talk to him in between scenes. I noticed the folded piece of paper – a torn piece of one of our play programs--sticking out from under my pillow as soon as I entered my room.

L. Never mind what we said before – I just can't. I'll pick it up during the play. We might not have a chance to talk. Meet me at the train at 11:30 or if something seems wrong meet me at home where we found the big snapping turtle. Don't draw attention to yourself. Love, B.

I was relieved that Billy was unable to go through with killing Thomas, as well. We would perform the play as if nothing was unusual. I wanted to tell the authorities about Thomas. Billy wanted to take the box and just leave. I suppose he thought that Thomas would then live out the rest of his life in terror knowing we were out there, knowing we had the evidence that could have him arrested or even hanged. Maybe he would never even know that we were the children of the man he killed. Maybe it was better that he didn't. Never knowing exactly why we did what we did or where we were or if we were looking for him might be more of a punishment than any prison.

I shoved the note that Billy had written me into the only place I could think of – the heating grate – so that I had no evidence that we had planned anything. I packed my things in my bag and put my bag in the closet. This was the only performance of the show, so it didn't seem too unusual that an actress had packed her things in preparation to leave, I hoped. I headed over to the Opera House to get ready. I saw Billy for just a moment to make sure that we truly understood one another. I was elated that we did. Billy said that during second act – during Thomas' biggest scene--he would go back to Mrs. Twilly's, grab the box and hide it in the storage closet behind the stage until after the play. After the final curtain, we could change, grab our things and head to the station as if we were merely heading home for a visit. Thomas would certainly be distracted by adoring fans wanting to talk to him until well into the night. Since we had three days before we were to show up in Trenton to begin practice on a new play, our leaving would seem perfectly logical. We would even make certain to say good-bye to Thomas and Virginia. We didn't think Thomas would really have any reason to look for the box under his bed until the next morning when we knew he was to leave, or at the very earliest, much later in the evening after we had already gone.

As the audience gathered for the play, Billy got ready for his entrance on the far side of the stage. The curtain rose and both of us waited for Virginia and Thomas to enter from Billy's side of the stage. I

191

could see Virginia shaking her head and moving her hands in a worried fashion as she talked to Billy. Virginia and Thomas should have been on stage by now, and I could see John Howell, the director, standing up from his seat in the front row, making his way to Billy's side of the stage embarrassedly. After a moment, Mr. Howell took center stage and said, 'I am so sorry folks, but it seems that Mr. Madden, the man who plays Matthew Carbuncle, is not here as of yet. Miss Kellogg assures me that nothing like this has ever happened before, so we are greatly concerned that something may have happened to him. We would be happy to refund your money or give you tickets to another upcoming show. If you would be so inclined, please wait patiently for a few minutes. It is possible that Mr. Madden is simply running a bit late. We are so sorry for the inconvenience.'

Billy told Mr. Howell that he would go to the boarding house and see if Thomas was there. That was the last I saw of Billy that night.

Most of the audience stayed in their seats for about fifteen minutes, and then gradually, some started drifting toward the ticket office to get refunds or rain checks for tickets. Virginia looked confused, Mr. Howell looked angry, and I felt worried. Still, I thought, it was best to stay put.

When Billy didn't come back to the theater or the boarding house and Thomas was nowhere to be found, I decided not to go to the train stop, but instead to spend the night so that I appeared to be just another perplexed person in the town of Beech Grove. That's exactly how I tried to present myself at ten minutes after midnight when the police came to talk to me.

I had tiptoed across the floor of my room, trying hard not to make the floor squeak when I heard the doorbell ring. I heard the police and Mrs. Twilly conversing quietly. From the crack in my bedroom door I understood that Mr. Madden, dressed in women's clothes, was found dead behind the train stop a few minutes earlier. Mrs. Twilly told them that she had seen Mr. Madden, dressed as a woman, come down the steps and head in the direction of the train stop, away from the Opera House, at the time the play would have been about to begin. She thought it terribly strange, but didn't particularly think it merited a call to the police.

The police asked to speak with me and I went down after Mrs. Twilly knocked on my door. When asked if Mr. Madden's part required him to dress as a woman, I told them that it did not, and that I had no idea why he would have been dressed in that manner. The two men asked me a series of questions – How long had I known Mr. Madden? (About a year) Was he often prone to such odd behavior? (No) Did he have any enemies? (None that I knew of) Did he have a family? (His mother had died years ago. He was not married and had no children. I didn't know of any other relatives.)

They thanked me graciously, and asked to speak to Billy and Virginia. I told them that I was certain that Billy would be happy to answer their questions, but he wasn't home. When they looked at me as if they found that fact very interesting, I calmly explained that Thomas and Billy were like brothers, and that when Thomas hadn't shown up for the performance we were all very concerned. Billy had gone in search of Thomas and was probably still scouring everywhere he could think of.

The answer must have seemed logical to the two officers, because they thanked me again and asked to speak with Virginia. Virginia answered their questions and flirted with the policemen for more than twenty minutes. When they left, they had no more knowledge than they had when they had walked in. Virginia, for once in her life, proved useful in the way she distracted the police.

At 6:00 a.m. the next morning, I went to Billy's room unsure of what I would find. Billy wasn't there, but his case, like mine, had been packed and was standing inside the closet door. He must have packed it before the cancelled performance. His bed had not been slept in, which I guess I expected, because I was certain that if he had come back, he would have come to my room to speak to me.

I formed a story in my head as I went down to breakfast with Mrs. Twilly and Virginia. I knew I had to tell a lie, possibly several, to protect Billy. I wasn't absolutely certain though, that Billy was in trouble. My heart had been thudding wildly in my chest since the first strange incident of Thomas not appearing for the show. That coupled with the fact that I hadn't slept during the night because I was listening for any sign of Billy, was taking its toll on me. I worked hard at doing exactly what Billy had told me to do in the note – not draw attention to myself.

After breakfast I told Mrs. Twilly and Virginia that I was going to go for a walk. I left for almost an hour to gather my thoughts. I walked into the wooded area behind Mrs. Twilly's house. The fewer people who saw me, the better. When I came back I began to tell the small, but important lies that could protect Billy. I told Mrs. Twilly that I had found Billy on my walk coming back from the north side of town. I told her that he had been walking all night searching everywhere that Thomas might be. I told her that he had been devastated at the news of Thomas' death when I told him. I said that he asked me to come back and grab his things. He was too upset to speak with anyone right now. I told Mrs. Twilly that it was fortunate that Billy, Virginia and I had a few days to recover from this tragedy before deciding what to do next without Thomas. Virginia had chirped in and made the most gracious offer of her life – to make the arrangements for Thomas' burial. She had nowhere to go for the next few days, anyway. We decided that since Thomas really had no family or home that we knew of, it would make sense to have him buried in Beech Grove. The gratitude I felt toward Virginia for the first and probably only unselfish act she would ever perform, was immense. I thanked Virginia and told her that we should meet in a few days in Trenton. I paid Mrs. Twilly for Billy's room and mine and offered to pay for Thomas' as well.

That's when Mrs. Twilly said something unusual. She told me that Thomas had left payment for his room and the most generous tip she had ever received on his bed when he left.

Thomas had indeed intended to leave quietly when no one was around. Suddenly I realized that not only did I not know where Billy was, I didn't know where the box was either. If Thomas had left in a hurry, he certainly would have taken it with him, but the police made no mention of any items found with Thomas' body. Could Billy have it? Could it still be under the bed?

I thanked Mrs. Twilly and went upstairs to grab both my bag and Billy's. At the top of the stairs I quickly went into Thomas' room first and bent down to look under the bed. Nothing.

Where was Billy and where was the box?"

195

"I swear this is a motion picture deal waiting to happen!" Mom blurted as she shook her head back and forth, stunned. "A cross-dressing actor on the run from the children of the man that he murdered while robbing a bank—you can't make this kind of thing up!"

"Can you imagine how scared Olivia had to be? She'd already lost her father and her husband. Her mother had moved, and now her brother might be in big trouble!" Katie said sadly. Her words reminded everyone around the table that this was real, not just a made up story. These events had really happened to someone, even though it was very long ago.

Mrs. Portage continued reading.

"I grabbed our bags and headed to the train stop. No one but Mrs. Twilly and Virginia expected that Billy and I were leaving together. Fortunately, on the streets of the town, even though it was quite a small one, I was just another face. I calmly bought my ticket (and one for Billy, just for the sake of appearances) to Rosewood.

The train made several stops. From the window I looked for some sign that Billy had made it this far – that he was in front of me leading the way to the pond where we had found the big snapping turtle years ago. The pond where the note said to meet if things seemed suspicious. This certainly qualified.

The train stopped at the station on Main Street in Rosewood. I was almost home. This was the first time I had been here in over a year. The feeling of relief that I perhaps should have felt was overshadowed by the fear that I wouldn't find Billy. I began to walk down Birch Street toward Magnolia Street that leads out of town. It was almost a mile walk from the center of Rosewood to the outskirts where our farm was, especially long wearing heels and carrying two bags. As I suspected, a generous soul offered me a ride and I gratefully accepted.

I suddenly realized at the gate to the farm how much could change in only a year. Benny had told me when I had called home at Christmas, that Mr. Dixon, my father-in-law, had died the week before. I had had no reason to come home for the funeral of the man who had treated my husband so poorly, so I chose not to. Benny told me that Mr. Dixon had left him and Edmund's siblings the farm. They had eagerly accepted when Benny offered to buy the farm from them. Benny was in the process of combining both farms into one, under one name – 'Taters.' That was the name on the large wrought-iron sign hanging on the gate to my newly-expanded family farm.

I thanked the man that had given me the ride and walked toward the house I had grown up in. I walked around the side and back by the barn, still carrying the cases. I was grateful that there was no one, not a soul, around. When I could see the pond, I felt an unbelievable need to run, as if time was about to run out. I kicked off my shoes, dropped the bags and ran as fast as I could to the pond.

There, under the oak tree was Billy, breathing heavily. It looked like he was asleep. When I got to him, it was not relief I felt, but terror. His was not the breathing of someone sleeping, but someone dying. When I whispered his name, he opened his eyes and tried to sit up. I helped him prop himself up slightly against the tree. That's when I saw the blood still silently oozing from his right side. It seemed like more blood than could be held in a single human body.

'I knew you'd make it,' Billy said with a weak smile.

'I'm going for the doctor,' I said starting to stand.

My little brother, now a man, grabbed me by the arm and said in a voice that could not be disobeyed, 'You won't, Liv. Sit down and listen to what I have to say.'

I did so without a word.

'I killed Thomas, but truly, it was an accident. You need to know that. I went to the boarding house to find him, and he was already gone. I had checked his room – he had taken all his clothes and the box. I knew he had headed toward the train. I ran after him and found him. He must have had that disguise with him for years, just in case. No one else was on the street or near the train stop; even the old man that gave out the tickets had closed the window. I told Thomas we needed to talk. It was

197

my idea to go behind the station. Honestly, Liv, I just wanted to talk to him. I wanted there to be some explanation, something I had overlooked. I didn't want him to be our father's killer. So I started at the beginning. I told him it might sound crazy – I said this to a man in a dress, mind you – but I thought that he might be the man that killed my father in a bank robbery five years earlier. I told him that I had been following his career ever since he and the theater troupe had come to Rosewood in a play about a year after Dad had been killed. He said nothing, so I just kept talking. I told him that I didn't want it to be him--that it couldn't be him, because I knew no killer would go back to the same town out of the simple fear of being recognized and caught. Thomas remained silent, staring at me, and I began to ramble on to him about how I had been coming to walk with Dad home from the bank the day he was killed. I told him that I had seen the killer – and it looked like him. I told Thomas simply that I wanted to be wrong. I told him, though, that I had seen the box, the box that I was certain was in the big suitcase in his hand. I said that I wanted an explanation, something. After that we could decide what to do.

Thomas opened his mouth as if to say something – the look on his face was one of regret, but then suddenly it changed. His mouth shut and he pulled the gun from out of a pocket in the dress. He said nothing. He simply shot me. I lunged forward and shoved him. I don't know what I intended to do, but I pushed him. His heels and his bad leg caused him to fall. He hit his head on a rock beside the road and died instantly. I almost grabbed his ticket and got on the train, but I knew that the old man would have remembered selling it to him and that the police would notice it was gone. They would also have noticed if I took the suitcase, so I didn't. I took the box from inside it and the gun and headed out of town quickly, hoping no one had heard the shot. I got a ride in the back of a pickup full of hay with a farmer, and made it almost all the way here. The gun is in the pond.'

'Why won't you let me get the doctor? Why didn't you get help? People would understand that he killed your father – that what happened when Thomas fell was an accident!' I practically screamed.

'Would they, Liv? Or would they think I was just a guy out for revenge? Would they really be wrong? I'm not willing to take the chance that people would believe the truth, when I'm not even really sure what the truth is.' Billy's voice was weaker, but still resigned to his choice.

He handed me an envelope in his blood-stained hand. 'Read it. I found it in the box.'

I could tell by the bloody fingerprints on the envelope and the letter inside that he already had.

Right there, in black and white, were the answers both of us had been searching for.

It read, 'This is my confession. I, Thomas Madden, robbed the Rosewood Savings and Loan on June 8*th*. I escaped with over $8000 in cash, a safety deposit box containing bonds and a diamond necklace. It was not my plan to injure anyone. I needed the money to pay off my gambling debts. When the bank teller gave me the money, I demanded the box on the counter so that I could put the cash inside. He was looking for the key to it when a woman came in and screamed and startled me and the gun went off. I had chosen this bank to rob because my troupe had performed in a play in this sleepy town months earlier. I watched the bank to see when there were few customers and when tellers went to lunch. I had planned to give the money to the man that had been threatening me the very next day, but I heard from an acquaintance after the robbery that he had been sent to prison only a day or two before. It made me sick that I had killed a man to save my own skin. I broke the box open and put the money inside. It goes everywhere I go – I guess as a constant reminder of my sins. I'll never spend a penny of it. I can't.'

'You were right, Billy.' I said looking from the letter to my little brother.

'Live a good life, Liv.' Billy said pointing up toward the big hole in the tree he was leaning against – the tree where Daddy and Benny had hung the swing so long ago. He took a final breath, and died. I held his blood-stained hand and looked at his face, finally peaceful. A face that seemed to say that he had found all the answers."

Chapter 41

Mrs. Portage had stopped reading. The words couldn't come out through her stifled sobs. Katie could barely see through all the tears streaming from her eyes. Dad had his hands on his head, his elbows on the table and was shaking his head back and forth. Mom was on the phone, explaining to the frantic bride-to-be that something urgent had come up and Mom would have to meet her later.

"Um hm…Yes I know the most important day of your life is fast approaching, but there is a very important day in my daughter's life that is already here. Yes, 11:00 will be fine."

Mrs. Portage pushed the journal across the table to Katie, and as she did, something behind the last page of the journal became slightly visible. Katie pinched it and pulled it gently out. It was the blood-stained envelope that Katie was sure held the confession of Thomas Madden. The very letter that Billy handed Olivia under the oak tree by the pond.

Katie opened it and passed it to Mrs. Portage. She read it and passed it to Dad while Katie took up reading where Mrs. Portage had left off. Katie turned to the next page.

"I told Benny the entire story — from start to finish — except for where the box was hidden. That was my other lie, and to be honest, the only reason I can think that I told it was because I felt that the box had caused us enough anguish already.

Benny and I thought it best to bury Billy here on the farm. No one needed to know. Billy had kept to himself growing up, and that, we thought, might prove to be an asset to us. We told those who asked that Billy had gotten a job with another traveling theater group and was working out west for much better pay. I contacted Virginia and told her that Thomas' death had been too much for Billy and me and that we wanted to stop acting. She was relieved because she had been offered a part in a play in Cleveland that she hoped would lead to big things."

Another entry, "*I have spent almost a week alone in the house that I built with Edmund. The grief I feel at the loss of Billy is slightly lightened by the knowledge that he found what he set out to find.*"

And then the final entry, "*I am going back. I know that like Thomas Madden, I have no desire to ever spend, let alone see, what is in the box. It still sits in the hole in the tree by the pond where Billy placed it. I want someone to know.*

If what I am planning to do actually works, you will have found my journal in the floor of the boarding house — perhaps merely by accident. I am going back to put it there because I want the past buried in a place where someone, just an average, ordinary person may someday stumble upon it. That may never happen if my book is in a hole, decaying in the ground. I am planning to visit Mrs. Twilly and ask her if I may take a look at the room I stayed in over a decade ago. I hope I am graceful enough to get her to leave me alone for a few minutes in the room so that I can hide the journal under the loose floorboard. I plan to give her my copy of Now and Then *to add to her collection. If you haven't found the script yet, there's no need, my story is all here. I am leaving Billy's note to me where I hid it in the heating grate. I don't know why, but I thought that these clues might lead someone clever to my story.*"

That was it. The end of the journal. Not another word, not another sketch. Katie closed the book and gently slid the leather strap into the loop.

Everyone was silent. The mystery had been solved. Katie felt a rush of both sadness and relief. So did Mom, Dad and Mrs. Portage. Katie could see it on their faces.

"So, I guess there is only one thing left to do," Mrs. Portage said.

"Call Skip and donate the journal to the historical society?" Katie asked, her thoughts a jumble with Olivia's story.

"Good idea, little one. But don't you think first we should go on a little field trip?"

Mom was excited and grumpy at the same time—a very strange combination. She wanted to go with Katie, Dad, Neil and Mrs. Portage, but the bride-to-be had already been rescheduled once today. Mom knew that if she did that again, she would probably lose out on making all the food for the stressed-out woman's wedding. As much as Mom wanted to go with them, she thought that it was equally important to look after her business. She made Dad swear that he would call her the moment they learned or discovered anything. Dad had to agree eleven different times before Mom would move from the doorway to let them get in the van.

As Dad drove, Katie re-read many of the entries in the journal out loud. Mrs. Portage sat quietly listening in the front seat. Neil slept peacefully in his car seat—a fact for which Katie was immensely grateful.

An hour later, they were on Main Street in Rosewood. The town, Katie was sure, had grown greatly since Olivia had been here last. Dad remembered that Olivia had mentioned Magnolia Street in the journal. In no time, they found themselves parked in front of a large iron gate overrun with weeds outside of town. The sign that said "Taters" hung sideways, swinging from one bolt. The lock had been broken and in the breeze the gate hinges squealed.

Katie, in her haste to leave, had forgotten her notebook that in the course of the week had gotten quite stuffed with facts, copies and notes. She tried hard to remember what she knew about the "Taters'" owner. He was a hard worker, a farmer, and the brother of Olivia and Billy. He had gotten his diploma in the 1970's and had been Ohio's oldest graduate. Katie hadn't thought about it before, but if Benjamin was in his seventies in the nineteen seventies, he had to be over one hundred years old now. Chances were pretty good, especially based on the look of the run-down gate that he had died long ago. Katie remembered that this was the farm listed on the Wyethville website that had had lots of activities—a corn maze, potato digging, pumpkin picking—but that the website had seemed outdated, perhaps not that outdated, though. Benny's family, or someone else, must have kept the farm running for quite a while. Katie felt disheartened to see all Benny's hard work in ruins.

There seemed to be no one to ask for permission, so Dad pushed the gate open far enough for Katie and Mrs. Portage to fit through. Neil and Dad followed. Katie remembered that Olivia had said which way she had gone the day that Billy had died, so she looked for the farmhouse and headed toward it. In just a few minutes, the pond was in view. Katie started toward it and realized that she was practically running. Mrs. Portage was walking at a fast clip, trying to catch up, but Dad and Neil had stopped.

"Come on, Dad. We've gotta see. . ."

"This is your adventure, Katie. We'll wait here."

Katie waited for Mrs. Portage to catch up, and together they headed toward the tree — the tree from the sketch in the script, the tree that showed up over and over again here and there in the journal.

Once she was right beside the trunk, Katie was certain she had never seen such an enormous tree in all of her life. The hole was a bit higher than the top of her head. Katie had always been afraid of bees, wasps and hornets. There could be a nest of some sort in there. Katie listened, but heard no buzzing. Even if she had heard something, she thought that reaching her hand into the hole would have been worth the risk.

Katie and Mrs. Portage waited a long moment — looking back and forth from each other to the hole. Finally, Mrs. Portage said what Katie had been thinking.

"You know, even if there is nothing there, it's really not a big deal. We solved the mystery. Isn't it amazing to think that we have the solution to a crime that happened almost a century ago — answers that no one else found. My, what an amazing adventure this has been. We will have such stories to tell!"

Katie nodded. She agreed completely. The box didn't matter at all. . . .but still, it would be nice.

Katie reached in expecting, hoping, to feel the hard square edges of a security deposit box like the one she had seen her mom place Grandma's emerald earrings in at the Beech Grove Bank. What she felt was soft. At first she thought it might be a dead bird, and immediately pulled her hand back. Finding what they were looking for was even worth touching a dead bird, so Katie tried again. It wasn't anything dead at all. It was a piece of cloth, a blanket. Katie pulled the tattered covering out of the hole and reached back in. The cold flatness against her hand almost made her black out.

Chapter 42

It was all there—the money, the necklace, even the bonds. All of it protected from the snow, the rain and the sun by a box, a blanket and a tree for almost ninety years.

Mrs. Portage was right. It wouldn't have really mattered if the box had not been there, but it certainly was a wonderful feeling to be holding the large, heavy final piece of the puzzle.

There had never been any doubt what they would do when they found the box—they turned it in to the authorities. The Beech Grove police chief listened awe-struck as Katie told the story. It was the most fascinating thing that had happened in the small town since the day that the mysterious man dressed as a woman had died from a hit on the head.

Chief Slone called the local paper. Ms Limbaucher was at the station in a matter of minutes and listened raptly as Katie animatedly told the story again.

Katie couldn't believe the amount of notice kids took of her at school on Tuesday. While she was gone on Monday, word spread like crazy of Terror Talia, as she was now known. Katie hadn't realized that Hunter had been in the store that day. He had seen the entire thing from Katie defending herself (and Hunter) to the punch in the back. Hunter had been ready to jump in and attack, as was his usual form, but Mr. McKeever beat him to it. Hunter made sure that everyone knew exactly what had happened—with a few embellishments that Katie didn't exactly mind. In Hunter's version of things, Talia had been handcuffed and sent to the detention home for a month. None of the students could be sure if this was true or not since Talia hadn't been at school on Monday, and she hadn't shown up so far today.

Whatever happened now with Talia didn't bother Katie a bit. She knew that other people now knew how Talia really acted. She knew that other people like Mr. McKeever, and even Hunter, were looking out for her. She just hoped that someday Talia would figure out what it meant to be a friend.

After school, Katie stopped to see Mrs. Portage and have a cookie. They both knew that in the last week they had started a new after school ritual that both of them thoroughly enjoyed. Mrs. Portage loved hearing about what all Katie's friends had asked and said about the mystery. She was thrilled when Katie asked her to come to school. Mrs. Tyler, the principal, had said that it was an amazing feat to solve a crime, and she wanted to have Katie and Mrs. Portage presented with an award in front of the entire school for community service.

The mystery that had consumed Katie for over a week had come to a close. Right now, she was the center of attention, and to be honest, Katie didn't mind in the least. Katie also knew that the excitement and interest would eventually die down. And that was all right. Katie knew what really mattered—having a family that loved her, being a good friend, and doing what was right. If that made her the odd one out, she'd take odd any day.